The Psychic Barista

The Brown Bean Coffee Shoppe

TIM TROTT

Tim Trott Publishing

Contents

Dedication

I dedicate this book to the members of the Daytona Beach writers' group (FWA), and in particular, Veronica Helen Hart (*Silent Autumn, Murder in Myrtle Beach*, etc.), who challenged me to write fiction, and Chris Holmes, who suggested expanding the initial *Coffee Plots* short stories into a collection.

I also dedicate this book to my wife, Marianne, who has always believed in my writing.

Chapter One

Dreamscape

Long shadows stretched ominously across the rough pavement as Samantha Wilson sprinted down an unfamiliar street, her heart pounding. Her pulse quickening at the sound of echoing footsteps that sent chills racing down her spine. She glanced over her shoulder. Panic surged through her veins. Had she escaped her pursuer? Her legs seemed like they were moving in slow motion. She had to go faster to get away.

Sam scanned her surroundings in a frantic search for a way out. Ahead was an old hotel, and she turned to it as an escape. Years of abandonment and neglect left the once grand entrance deteriorated. Glass from the massive door lay in pieces on the floor. Stepping through the broken glass, she moved inside and felt the numbing chill of cold water soaking her feet.

When she glanced down, the reflection she saw was not her own face, but that of a stranger.

Sam stopped and whispered, "Who are you?"

Hearing footsteps and crunching glass behind her, she took a deep breath and hurried ahead through the shallow water. Reaching the other side, she darted up a stairway and crouched on a balcony. Her heart pounded as the dark stranger passed by below. The man looked up at the balcony where Sam was hiding. She soon realized the old building was not the sanctuary she had hoped for. All at once, she froze, caught in the icy stare of the man with the weathered face and a dark baseball cap staring up at her.

And as abruptly as it had begun, Samantha's ordeal ended.

She sat up in bed, sweat glistening on her forehead. Her familiar bedroom came into focus, and she hugged her knees, unable to erase the chilling experience from her mind, and the dark stranger with the predatory glare hunting her down. Her heart racing, she scanned her familiar surroundings for reassurance. Relief washed over her as she realized it was only a dream.

Why was the man chasing her? And who was the woman in the water's reflection? Most of all, how could she be dreaming someone else's nightmare?

Morning came all too soon. Still exhausted as she awoke, Sam took a quick shower and stuffed a stale cupcake in her mouth as she dressed for work. She glanced in the mirror and was relieved her eyes were not noticeably red.

Before leaving for work, she paused a moment to think about the disturbing nightmare. What did it mean?

Samantha Wilson's hazel eyes were her most captivating feature, reflecting curiosity and empathy. Her manner fit her job as a barista at the Brown Bean Coffee Shoppe in an older section of a town on the Georgia coast. The coffee shop occupied a storefront commercial space. Angled parking spaces lined the street, some marked with signs cautioning of a 15-minute time limit for carry-out orders. There was no drive-through window.

Inside, early morning sunlight bathed the dark wooden floors. The inviting aroma of ground coffee beans filled the air, blended with the tempting sweet scent of pastries wafting from under glass domes on the counter. The cash register was a modern replica of the type that might have been there in a bygone era.

Sam arrived at work and took her place behind the counter as the morning customers
spilled into the small shop. She busied herself
by filling orders until the late morning, when
only a few customers remained. As Sam began
bussing the tables, clearing them of empty coffee cups and crumpled napkins, she noticed a
young woman in a red coat walking toward the
order counter.

Samantha Wilson

Samantha turned to look more carefully. She
recognized the face. It was the face in the reflection in her dreadful dream.

Samantha returned to the sales counter. "What can we make for you this
morning?" Sam asked.

"I'd like a Grande almond milk latte with a shot of vanilla syrup, please,"
she said. The woman had dark hair and appeared slightly older than
Samantha. Sam studied the woman's face momentarily before turning to
complete the order.

As Samantha rang up the sale, the woman held her credit card over the
scanner. Sam tried to be inconspicuous as she angled her head to read the
name on the card: Georgiana Phillips.

"Do we know each other?" Samantha asked. "You seem familiar, somehow."

"I've only been in town a few weeks," the woman replied. "I'm a reporter
for channel 27."

"That must be it. I guess I saw you on TV!"

The woman smiled. As Samantha prepared the order, she had an uncomfortable feeling. She soon realized the reason when a man entered:
a man with a weathered face wearing a dark cap. Her heart sank as she
recognized him from her nightmare. All at once, she realized Georgiana
had to be the woman the man was stalking.

Sam handed Georgiana the latte and whispered, "I'm sure you think I'm crazy, us having just met and all, but I'm pretty sure someone followed you here."

Georgiana's expression shifted from curiosity to concern. "What do you mean? Who is it?"

"He came in after you and sat in the back. He is watching you now." Sam was careful not to look directly at the man. "Have you had any, you know, nasty comments on your social media, scary emails, things like that?"

"Well, yes, but in my job that often comes with the territory." She paused. "But some of them have been a *little* scary, now that you mention it. You say you've seen him before?"

This would be the challenging part. Samantha didn't want to reveal the real reason and decided on a different strategy. Instead, she framed her concern more broadly, focusing on Georgiana's safety and privacy.

"I don't want to scare you, but I think you should be very aware of your surroundings. Be careful when you are alone. You know, watch your back, look for a way out, that sort of thing." Samantha advised.

"I think you *are* scaring me, but I welcome your concern, and I will keep your advice in mind."

Samantha briefly turned to look.

"He's still there."

"What does he look like?" Georgiana asked.

"Well, for one thing, he's the only one in the room right now without coffee. He's in the back, wearing a dark baseball cap. But don't let him know you see him."

Georgiana stole a quick glance at the stranger, then with the latte cup in hand, she waved to Sam as she left the coffee shop. Once outside, she drove off in the TV news van. Sure enough, the strange man soon got up and left behind her.

At the end of her shift, Sam left by the back door to the employee parking lot and got in her car. As she reached the main street, she encountered road work and stopped traffic. She followed the detoured traffic down an alley and onto a street in a rough part of town.

Ahead, she saw the Channel 27 news van next to a large sign at a construction project. Georgiana stood in front of a camera, doing what television reporters call a "remote stand-up" for the afternoon news break.

Then Sam noticed something else.

As she slowed, her eyes detected movement ahead. A man wearing a dark baseball cap was watching the reporter from behind a parked car. Sam pulled her car in behind the news van and got out to wait for Georgiana to complete her broadcast. Facing Georgiana, her eyes obscured by dark sunglasses, Sam observed the man in the distance. She was now certain he was the same as the man in the coffee shop. More importantly, it was also the man in her nightmare.

Georgiana finished the report and beckoned Samantha to come forward.

Sam smiled, lowering her head as she approached, and whispered, "Please don't turn around, but that guy from the coffee shop is watching you again. I have a very bad feeling."

Georgiana whispered back, "What should we do?"

Samantha smiled, then covering her lips with her hand, she said, "I have a plan if you're up to it. I'm hoping he doesn't want to confront both of us, so we'll stay here. I'll

Georgiana Philips, Reporter

get 9-1-1 on my phone. When I'm sure the police are listening, and before your stalker gets any closer, we'll have a little conversation and let the police know about the situation and our location."

Georgiana nodded in cautious agreement. "My camera is still on. The studio crew can see me, and hopefully, they'll hear what's going on."

Samantha pretended to be casually answering a text message as she dialed 9-1-1. The menacing stalker remained impatiently in the shadows as the two women pretended to be in a friendly conversation. Sam softly described the stalker hiding behind a car on the next block. Georgiana described their situation on her studio mic and added the location for the police listening on Samantha's phone. The girls continued their conversation.

Many long minutes later, Sam smiled and nodded, looking over Georgiana's shoulder as an unmarked car with two police officers pulled up in the distance. One officer went to the far side of the street, and the other approached the menacing stalker from behind.

Still focused on the women, the stalker pulled out a long knife, gripping it in his fist as if preparing to leap forward. In an instant, the police made their move. Seeing the first officer approach from the side, the stalker turned, only to face the other officer behind him. After a brief struggle, the stalker was subdued, cuffed, and placed in the back of the police car. One officer stayed with the prisoner while the other approached the two women.

"Are you two OK?" the officer asked. Seeing their relief, he continued. "That was clever, the way you described your situation for the 9-1-1 operator. Lucky for you, we were working the traffic on the next block. At first, we were going to ask that guy what he was doing, but when he pulled a knife, we had probable cause to stop him. The station told us about nasty messages on social media. The threats might tie back to this guy."

Wiping her brow in relief, Georgiana spoke up. "It's like a bad dream." She stopped, turned to Samantha, and asked, "But how did you know?"

Samantha replied, "I'll tell you about it sometime. Maybe over a nice latte?"

Chapter Two

Dangerous Brew

Samantha Wilson's day had started out like any other. By mid-morning, the takeout customers had slowed to a trickle. She had her back turned to the sales counter when she had a disturbing and uneasy feeling. She turned to see an older woman with a young, dark-haired girl. The girl seemed jittery.

"Good morning! What can I make for you two?" Sam asked with a smile.

"I'll have a plain coffee, to go," the woman snapped. Noticing Sam's glance toward the girl, she continued, "Only the one coffee."

Sam sensed fear in the young girl. They locked eyes, and the girl's gaze darted toward the woman. Samantha felt she was trying to communicate something.

Samantha prepared the order, rang up the sale, and they went to sit at a corner table. A short time later, a well-dressed man came in and sat at the table with them. After a brief exchange, all three left together.

A few minutes later, Samantha's new friend Georgiana arrived for her "usual."

With a nod from Georgiana, Samantha grabbed a cup to prepare the Grande almond milk latte with a shot of vanilla syrup.

"What's bothering you today?" Georgiana inquired, her keen reporter's eye catching subtle signs from her friend.

Sam rang up the sale and shrugged. "I'm not sure. A customer came in earlier with a teen, a girl, but something about them gave me a chill."

Georgiana asked, "In what way?"

"The girl was afraid. I just felt it," Sam replied. "The woman only bought a coffee for herself—nothing for the girl."

Georgiana turned to make sure there was no one in line behind her. She hesitated momentarily before leaning in to say, "We produced a special report on human trafficking. I wonder if that was what you sensed?"

"Perhaps. But what can we do?" Sam asked.

Georgiana thought for a moment. "I know someone we can ask." With that, she gave Samantha a wink, picked up her order, and left the coffee shop.

Later, near the end of Samantha's shift, Georgiana returned with a man wearing a light brown suit.

"Back for another latte?" Sam asked when the pair entered.

"Not this time," she said, turning to her guest. "I want you to meet Detective Ronald Johnson. He was my source for the report on human trafficking I told you about."

Detective Ronald Johnson, a seasoned investigator with the city Police Department, showed the effects of years spent chasing criminals on his weathered face.

The detective greeted Samantha.

"Georgiana mentioned you had concerns about something you saw this morning?"

She nodded and directed her guests to an empty table.

Yes," Sam replied. "Something about the woman and the young girl gave me a chill. I think the girl was afraid of the woman, but I could have been imagining it."

Detective Ronald Johnson

"Not necessarily," the detective cautioned. "What made you feel the girl was afraid? Did she make eye contact with you?"

Samantha nodded. "Yes, but only briefly. I thought she was trying to send me a message."

"I see." The detective continued. "The girl's reaction may have been a sign. Victims of human trafficking can appear anxious. The fact the woman bought nothing for the girl might be suspicious. Have they been here before?"

"Not that I can remember," Samantha told the detective. "But I have this feeling they'll be back. What should I do?"

"I see security cameras. Does the coffee shop have monitoring?" the detective asked.

"Marge, the manager, told me they have off-site video recording. And we have a bill trap in the register. Removing the secret bill sends an alarm signal to the security service. That way, we don't risk being seen pushing a button."

"That's a good system," Detective Johnson responded. "Tell you what, I'll get the name and number of the security company from your manager. We'll contact the company and let them know that a situation other than a robbery may trigger the alarm. They can report to me when they receive a hold-up signal."

He continued, "But don't take chances. If this is a human trafficking situation, we don't want you to put yourself or anyone else in danger. We don't need any heroes. Young girls and human traffickers can be a dangerous brew. These are not nice people, and if that young girl is a victim, we don't want to put her in any more danger than she already is. Understood?"

The women both nodded in agreement.

Detective Johnson handed Sam his card. "I'll alert my department to the situation."

That night, Samantha thought: *there must be something we can do.* She lay in bed for hours, trying to devise a plan.

By morning, she was ready. When she arrived at work, she wrote a note and hid it under the counter, out of sight.

The note read, "If you are the victim of human trafficking, go to the restroom and lock the door. Then, knock on the back employee door. Help will come."

If the woman returned, Sam's only problem would be passing the note without being noticed or putting the victim in danger.

In the afternoon, Samantha was worried her plan might be for nothing when she saw the same woman but with a different girl. This girl was a little older but had the same timid look as the one the day before. The woman again ordered a plain coffee and nothing for her young companion. The two took a seat at a table. An older gentleman seated at another table came over to join them. The man eyed the young girl and mumbled something to the woman.

Samantha's senses were on high alert. When she looked at the young girl, she sensed the girl was sending a thought message, "Help me!"

Sam reached into the cash drawer and slid the bait bill out from the secret bill trap. She palmed the note from under the counter and motioned for Marge to take over the register. Sam poured a glass of water, placed it on a tray, and draped a towel over her arm.

"I thought the young lady might like a glass of water," Sam said cheerfully. She placed the glass on the table near the girl and nudged it over, spilling it on her.

"Oh! I'm so sorry! How clumsy of me. Here, I'll clean it up." Samantha leaned down with the towel and soaked up the water on the table with one hand. With her other hand, she pressed the note into the girl's hand under the table.

"We have plenty of paper towels in the ladies' room," she said, looking up at the girl. "Why don't you go tidy up? Before the woman could object, the young girl got up and walked to the ladies' room, gripping the note tightly in her hand.

With the girl safe inside the women's restroom, Samantha told the woman she needed a mop to finish cleaning the floor. Once in the stockroom, she heard a knock. She unlocked the door and told the girl to wait in the stockroom.

As she returned to the table with the mop and pail, Marge was taking an order from a police officer at the front counter. The officer turned to face the woman's table. When the woman became nervous and got up from her chair, the older gentleman seated with her reached into his pocket to produce a badge. The officer at the counter stepped up and gripped the woman's arm.

The one officer restrained the woman in handcuffs and took her away. Samantha motioned to the other officer and guided him to the back storeroom.

When Detective Johnson arrived a short time later, Sam was sitting at a table, getting a grip on her nerves after the excitement.

"My officer told me what you did. You took a chance, young lady," he said, taking a seat at her table.

"I didn't know what else to do," Samantha said. "I sensed the fear in this girl, the same as the other one."

Detective Johnson smiled. "Your special senses were right on target. We connected with the trafficking ring through a social media post and had our undercover agent pose as a customer for the trafficker. The only problem we had was figuring out a way to separate the girl from her handler, but you solved that for us. I'm sure when we interrogate that woman, we will find the girl you saw before and possibly others."

A familiar face appeared. It was Georgiana in her red TV reporter's coat.

"I heard we might have a news story here," she said to the detective with a wink at Samantha. "Can we set up an interview when you have a conviction? That will make a nice follow-up for our story on the human trafficking problem."

Samantha turned to the detective and grinned.

"You never know what the two of us will brew up around here."

Chapter Three

The Face in the Cup

The afternoon sun painted streaks of sunlight across the tables inside the Brown Bean Coffee Shoppe. Samantha made a cup of coffee for herself, only her second of the day. With her afternoon break approaching, she gestured towards an empty table, signaling Marge, the manager, in the back. Marge nodded as Samantha poured a bit of cream.

Samantha brushed her chestnut-brown hair from her expressive hazel eyes as she walked to an empty table in the corner of the seating area.

Sam glanced at the coffee cup in her hand in shock as the swirls of cream formed the image of a woman with flowing hair. She closed her eyes and heard a beeping sound. She shook her head to clear her mind. When she opened her eyes, the sound was gone, but the face in the cup remained. Sam grabbed a spoon from the wall dispenser to stir away the image. But as she stirred, she had a strange feeling, as if the now distorted image was still reaching out to her in desperation.

She'd imagined it, she decided. Nothing more!

The bell over the doorway broke her thoughts as a customer went to the order counter. As Samantha went to assist the new customer, the television screen on the wall caught her attention.

"NEWS BULLETIN". The headline read "Abducted In Daylight Attack." The camera switched from the news anchor to Channel 27 field reporter Georgiana Phillips and a photo of the abduction victim.

Sam stared in shock, realizing she recognized the face framed by long hair. It was the face of the apparition in her coffee cup. On the TV screen, a news report identified the victim as the mayor's wife, Clara Stamford. Shaken, Sam gulped down the coffee and continued to the sales counter to help the customer.

Later, nearing the end of her shift, Sam hung up her apron in the storeroom and grabbed her purse from a shelf. At the front counter, her friend, Georgiana Phillips, was stopping by for an afternoon latte. Georgiana looked poised with authority, even off-camera, in her red jacket bearing the Channel 27 logo. In the news business, people would describe her as having "presence.

She deftly waved a few fingers toward Samantha as she paid Marge for the coffee.

"Are you in a hurry?" Sam asked, her voice raised a bit.

"No, I don't have another report until the six o'clock."

Sam said with some urgency, "I want to tell you about a strange experience I just had."

"What's up, Sam?" she asked with concern as she approached the corner table.

"That woman who was abducted, the mayor's wife..." she began.

"What about it? Do you know her?"

"No, I don't, and that's the problem. Just before I saw the news report on TV, I saw that woman's face in my coffee cup. I swear, it was the same woman. I had the strangest feeling. It scared me."

"Are you sure your eyes weren't playing tricks on you?"

"That's what I thought. I closed my eyes to make it go away, to shut it out of my mind, but when I did, I heard 'beep-beep-beep.' You know, like when a truck is backing up."

"You think I'm going to say you're crazy, right?" Georgiana responded.

Sam waited for the answer.

"Well, I'm not. I know you better than that," she continued as she took a chair across from Sam. "Let me tell you why. When I was an intern at the Atlanta station before I came here, we did a weekend special interest story about an organization that does research on remote viewing. Considering your history, just in the time I've known you, it wouldn't surprise me if you have another psychic ability at play here."

"How can that be if I don't even know what it is?" Sam asked.

Georgiana reached across the table and touched Samantha's hand to reassure her.

"In the interview, I learned certain people have an ability to visualize something at a distance using what you might know as ESP. Before you think it all sounds silly, there was an official government program that tried to use it to spy on our enemies in the Second World War, and it went on for years."

"Can it happen, just like that, like it did for me?"

"Well, no, not exactly. The process normally involves the 'receiver,' that's you, usually in a quiet and comfortable place, with as few distractions as possible. Except you seemed to have skipped the warm-up part. Anyway, they guide the viewer to what they call the target."

"Like the woman I saw in the cup?"

Georgiana nodded as she continued. "When we did the story, they set up an experiment as a demonstration. The viewer was told to imagine the contents of a sealed envelope. After a while, the remote viewer drew on a piece of paper. When they opened the envelope, there was a picture inside."

Sam blurted out, "And the picture matched the drawing? That is weird! Okay, so what about the sound?"

Georgiana nodded. "Sounds and even smells can be part of it."

"Okay, so what can we do about it?" Samantha asked.

Georgiana replied, "You could help the police solve another crime."

"Yeah, if you can convince them we're not both totally bonkers!"

"Let me talk to Detective Johnson about it. I think you made an impression on him when you helped catch that human trafficker and my stalker. I think he'll listen."

The next morning, before her midday shift at the station, Georgiana visited the police department. She spotted Detective Ronald Johnson in the hall and waved to get his attention.

The detective was a lifelong veteran of police work, having risen through the ranks after graduating from the police academy. His appearance was not laid back, but not imposing either. He looked the part of a police officer even without a uniform.

"Hey, what brings you here?" the detective asked when he saw Georgianna. "Is this official business?" he asked.

"Not really. Well, maybe not yet, anyway," she replied. "You remember my friend Samantha at the coffee shop, don't you?"

"Sure. Don't tell me she's ready to help solve another case for us."

"Don't laugh, but maybe. The kidnapping? Are you handling that case?" she asked.

"There are several of us working on it. It's a big one, being Mayor Stamford's wife and all."

Georgiana continued: "I'm going to ask you something that might seem strange. Have you ever heard of Remote Viewing?"

"I seem to recall something about it. Wasn't that some government project they had during the war? I don't remember the details. It seems like they had people trying to see what was going on in Russia or something like that," he answered.

"It might surprise you to know it's still going on. There's an organization called the International Remote Viewing Association in Atlanta," she said.

"So, what does that have to do with the mayor's wife?" Johnson asked.

"You know how Samantha seems to have this extra sense? Well, this morning, she saw the face of the mayor's wife in her coffee cup."

"You mean she imagined she saw her?"

"No, I mean, she saw a vision in the coffee cup before she knew anything about the kidnapping."

"Okay, let's say I want to go along with you on this, and I'm not saying I am, but what do we do about it?" the detective asked.

"When I was in Atlanta, we did a weekend feature story on an organization there. In the interview, they talked about their history, going back to the war, and then showed a remote viewing demonstration for my report. I have to tell you, it was amazing. Oh, and here's one clue: Samantha heard a beeping sound, like a truck backing up."

"That could mean a truck stop or a forklift in a warehouse. That could tell us something about where our victim is being held."

"Exactly!" Georgianna said with visible excitement. "Then you believe me!"

"I wouldn't go that far, at least not yet, but with the pressure on us to solve this case, I'm ready to try anything. This morning, there was a ransom note or more of a threat. I can't tell you anything about the note except to say we don't have any time to waste, and very few clues to go on."

"Sam also told me she could smell fresh lumber and salt air. Do those clues mean anything to you?"

"I think that gives me an idea where to start looking. Thanks for the tip."

The police set up surveillance at the Seaport warehouses. A drone launched to survey the area from above identified a vehicle parked at a vacant building next to a lumber shipping yard. Police traced the license plate to one of the possible suspects. From extended observation, they were fairly sure the suspect was working alone. They could hear the familiar sound of a forklift backing up in the lumber yard. The clues were coming together.

A car turned off the main highway and stopped at the Seaport security gate.

"Alpha, this is Bravo. We've got a Food Dash delivery for the subject location," came the call on the radio to the SWAT commander. "What do you want to do?"

"Can you switch out the driver for one of our people?" asked the commander.

"Will do," came the reply.

A few minutes later, the delivery car pulled up to the warehouse, and the driver went to the door. The door opened, and the man inside stepped out, looking from side to side. As he exchanged a wad of bills for the bag of food, the "delivery driver" pulled out a gun from his back pocket and displayed a badge. "We need to talk," the officer said. The surprised suspect dropped the food bag and slowly raised hands in surrender.

As the suspect was being detained, the SWAT commander shouted, "Charlie, you have a go for the rescue. Go, go, go!" into the radio.

Silently, the police entered the building from the other side. Less than a minute later came the message: "Victim secured, building clear."

The SWAT team emerged from the warehouse with the mayor's wife. Officers guided a disheveled but relieved mayor's wife to a police car for transport to the hospital and a check-up.

After clearing the crime scene, Detective Johnson arrived and called Georgianna. "If you and your camera can be at the Seaport down by the docks, we'll have something for your next report. I'll arrange for the guards to let you through the gate."

"Will you be there?' asked Georgianna.

"Yeah, I'll still be filling out reports, gathering evidence, talking to witnesses in the area. You know, all the fun stuff."

"I'll check with my news director and see you in about twenty minutes."

Less than twenty minutes later, Georgiana Phillips appeared in her bright red Channel 27 windbreaker. She caught up with Detective Johnson to get the details of the story. Standing in front of a camera, microphone in hand, she was ready for her feed to the studio.

On cue, she began: "This is Georgiana Phillips, with a story that has a happy ending. Earlier, we reported the abduction of the mayor's wife from her home. But earlier today, the police rescued Sheila Stamford from the building behind me. A suspect is in custody, and after being checked at the hospital, Mayor Stamford's wife will be on her way home, safe and sound. I'm Georgiana Phillips, Channel 27 news, at the Seaport lumber yard."

The red light on the TV camera went off, and Georgianna walked to where Detective Johnson was talking with his officers.

"Thanks again for the news tip," she said with a wide grin.

"Thanks to Samantha. And to think it all came together from a face in a coffee cup."

Chapter Four

The Jogger

By one o'clock, Samantha was at the end of her shift and ready to head home, when a dark-skinned young man wearing a white t-shirt and khaki shorts raced through the front door of the Brown Bean.

The terrified look on the man's face startled her.

"Can I help you?" Samantha asked.

The panicked man didn't answer. He turned to look behind him, then at Sam for a moment, before he continued running. Samantha watched as the man ran by her and out the back door.

Marge, the manager, looked up from closing out the front register for the next shift.

Seeing no one, she asked, "Who were you talking to?"

"The guy who came jogging through just now." Sam answered.

"What guy?"

"The jogger," Sam replied.

Marge cocked her head at Samantha with a concerned reaction. "I didn't see anybody."

Samantha ran her hand through her hair as she stared at the back door.

"I think I saw a ghost," she mumbled, mostly to herself. She couldn't shake the image of the man she saw, or thought she saw, running through the coffee shop.

"Go home and relax," Marge suggested. "You've had a long day."

Sam thought nothing more about it until she watched the local evening news. According to the reporter, three white men had confronted a young black man who was out jogging. They chased him down and held him at gunpoint. Then, the assailants shot and killed the young jogger. Oddly, the report said there had been no arrests.

Her heart stopped when they showed a picture of the victim. She instantly recognized the tall, young black man.

Sam was glad when Georgiana stopped by the coffee shop the next day. "Got a minute?"

"Sure, I don't have an assignment yet unless they call me. What's up?"

"I think I saw that jogger who got killed yesterday."

Georgiana was concerned. "Where did you see him?"

"Right here in the coffee shop. He ran in the front and out the back. He looked right at me."

"When was that?" Georgiana reverted to her skeptical reporter mode.

"Right after one o'clock, I think," said Sam.

"That's not possible. That's when he was killed, but it was ten miles from here. You must have seen a ghost."

"I'm glad you said that and not me," Sam continued. "They said on the news there were no arrests. How can that be? Did you ask Detective Johnson about it?"

"I called him right after it happened. Somebody else in the department is handling the case. Being the only black detective, I can understand why he wants to stay out of it. There's a lot of tension in the department right now, what with the current racial situation in the city." She continued, "Whoever you saw, did he say anything?"

"No. I think he wanted to tell me something, but he didn't. He looked right at me." Sam paused and shrugged. "I know, crazy talk."

"Hmm. I've learned not to doubt your visions. Let me see what I can do. I'm going to ask if the TV station will let me do an investigative report."

That afternoon after work, Samantha left the coffee shop and got in her car. She gasped when she saw the jogger's face in the rear-view mirror. Turning around to confront the intruder, she found the back seat was empty. However, when she turned back, the face was still in the mirror, and she heard a faint voice telling her, "Video! Get the video!"

And then the vision faded.

Sam grabbed her phone from her purse and frantically texted Georgiana. "Call me when you get off work."

Later, after the evening newscast, Georgiana called.

"What's up?" she asked.

"How about a news tip?" Samantha told her. "There's a video of the shooting. You need to find it!"

"What video? Who told you there was a video?"

"You'll have to trust me. All I can say is that there is a video, and we, I mean you, need to find it."

Georgiana may have had doubts, but she knew not to let them stand in her way.

"I think I know where I can start looking. I'll let you know what I find."

Some weeks later, Sam asked Georgiana, "What's going on with the jogger case? Have they arrested anybody yet?"

"That's what's frustrating. They're trying to say the shooting was justified, that it was in self-defense."

"How can that be?" Sam asked.

"That's what I wondered. I can't say for sure, but there seems to be some connection between the district attorney and the shooters. They brought in another prosecutor. It didn't change anything. The new prosecutor came to the same conclusion, saying the shooting was self- defense. Now, it looks like the state Attorney General's office might get involved. He's coming under pressure from the jogger's family. There's a grand jury investigating the District Attorney for not bringing charges in the case. We'll see what happens."

"What about the video?" Sam asked.

"No luck so far," Georgiana admitted. "But I'm still trying. I'll let you know when I find anything."

Months later, Georgiana almost ran into the coffee shop. Marge was at the register, and Samantha was clearing tables after the morning rush.

"Sam! I still don't know how you knew, but there *really was* a video recording of that jogger, being chased down and shot. I kept pressure on my sources, and it finally paid off. One of the guys who chased down the jogger recorded the whole thing. Can you believe it? And I got a copy of the video! I'm doing a special studio report for tonight's newscast." Georgiana raised both fists and exclaimed, "I get to do a studio report!"

Sure enough, that night, Georgiana revealed the video in her investigative report. The video showed the young black man being chased down and subdued by two men before being shot. Eventually, all three faced serious charges.

Samantha will always wonder why the jogger's ghost appeared to her at the coffee shop. [1]

---

1. (Note: This story is fiction, but it was inspired by a real criminal case. The descriptions in this story do not and are not intended to represent the facts of the case.)

Chapter Five

Friends in Low Places

Detective Ronald Johnson rarely visited the Brown Bean Coffee Shoppe on Saturday.

"Good morning, Detective," Samantha greeted him. "What brings you to our side of town this early?"

"I ran into an old friend from the police academy. This is Larry Miller," the detective explained. "He's taking time off from his job with the state patrol in Atlanta for the antique car show this weekend. He's got a classic Thunderbird."

"It's nice to meet you," Sam said. "I'm sure Detective Johnson will be having his usual cappuccino. What can we get for you?"

"Plain coffee," he said, ignoring the many other options. "Black."

All the while, Samantha sensed a strong negative energy from Detective Johnson's guest. The moment his eyes shifted away, refusing to meet hers, it raised Sam's suspicions. Beneath his calm exterior, Sam sensed Miller was hiding more than his expression let on.

When the orders were ready, Detective Johnson thanked Sam, and the pair left to meet the auto transport at the show.

As the day went on, Samantha couldn't shake the lingering sense of foreboding. She decided she needed to act on her instincts, or she might regret it later. When her special "abilities" had played a part in several investigations, the detective had shared his private number, perhaps for just this kind of situation. She felt compelled to relate her concerns.

She sent a text message: "Call me when you are by yourself."

"Hey, what's up?" he asked. "Larry was busy showing off his T-Bird, so I went looking at some of the other cars. It's like stepping back in time."

I apologize for the interruption, but when you and your friend arrived this morning, I sensed a negative aura about him, as if he were concealing something.

"Sam, you know I've come to respect your special gift, whatever it is. I've also known Larry for a long time, but I'll keep my eyes open for anything suspicious. Thanks for the tip."

Larry appeared to be negotiating with someone interested in his car.

After making a mental note of the Georgia tag number, Johnson opened the door to look inside.

"Enjoying the car show?" Larry asked.

"There are a lot of cars you don't see anymore. My dad had one of these. His was one of the few with an air condi-tioner. I remember it was a SelectAire. But I see this one was made by DynaCool. Is it an after-market brand?"

"Yeah, it's a South American brand. It's common in Cuba, which is where this car came from. Cuba is a gold mine of old cars from back before the embargo, and most of them are in great condition. I buy them from a guy who imports them to Mexico, and I take them to car shows like this one. There's a lot of bureaucracy involved, but it's totally legal. It's done all the time. I make a nice side income."

The explanation was logical. But what about Samantha's suspicions? What could he be hiding? The detective's mind went back to a 2019 Customs and Border Protection report of 230 pounds of marijuana found hidden in a 1957 Chevrolet Bel Air from Cuba. An x-ray scan of the gas tank revealed the drugs.

Detective Johnson recognized some dots. He had an idea how he might make them connect.

"Like I said, my dad had a car like this. What would you say if I wanted to buy it from you?"

Miller seemed nervous, but he tried to hide it.

"You don't want this car. It's hard to get parts. Besides, I already have a buyer."

"Tell you what, whatever they offered, I'll beat it by $100."

Miller was adamant. "I'm sorry, I can't sell you the car."

Now Detective Johnson was almost certain there was something Larry was hiding.

"OK, if you don't want to sell it to me, I understand. I think I'll be heading home."

With that, the Detective left the car show, but he didn't go home. He had some things he wanted to check out at the office.

Detective Johnson sat at the computer in his office, going through DMV records online. He found several cars registered to Larry Miller, all classic models from the 1950s, each one sold within a short time, all showing original registrations transferred from Mexico. He wondered if Miller might be involved in more than selling classic cars as a hobby.

Samantha's perception would not be enough to base a request for a warrant. How could he find out for certain?

Johnson picked up his phone and dialed.

"Dispatch, this is Johnson. I need a BOLO for an Observe and Report on a Georgia tag, BRI-276. Can you have those reports come directly to me? It's at the car show. When it leaves, I want to know where it goes. Send it to my phone. Thanks."

When he got the message about where the car turned up, it was what he was waiting for. He picked up his portable police radio.

"Dispatch, this is Johnson. I'm 10-51 to the body shop. I'm going to need backup, but they need to stay out of view until I make the call."

The streets were abandoned as Johnson pulled his unmarked car into position a short distance from the body shop. The location was just far enough away to remain unnoticed, but to provide a line of sight to the garage.

Lights around the edges of the roll-up door were a sign of activity inside.

Soon, a car pulled up outside the garage, and two men went to the side door. Johnson recognized the face of the person who opened the door. It was Larry Miller.

The detective's phone buzzed with a text message, approving his request for a search warrant.

It would take too much force to crash in the roll-up door, and the side door was steel, and likely bolted from the inside. If they made too much noise or took too long, they could lose any evidence inside.

But Johnson was ready with a plan. An unorthodox plan, but a plan. At the back of the body shop, he could see a commercial power panel with a big handle. Johnson called the backup officers to move in and take positions on either side of the door while Johnson made his way to the back of the building. He pulled the handle and turned off the power. The door opened and someone inside came out to check on the power and was immediately subdued as other officers rushed in with guns drawn. At that moment, Johnson switched the power back on. It was all over in a matter of seconds.

The modified gas tank lay on the floor. There, on the workbench, were twenty neatly stacked plastic bags containing what was likely to be cocaine. The police lab would later confirm it.

When Johnson joined the officers inside, they were putting handcuffs on Larry Miller, who was clearly surprised by Johnson's presence when he appeared.

"You have some friends in low places," the detective said to his old friend as the officers took him into custody.

Once again, gambling on Samantha's special insight helped Detective Ronald Johnson solve another case.

Chapter Six

A Novel Investigation

Marge walked up to the register where Samantha was working. With a nod toward an older woman seated at a table by the front window, she leaned in and whispered, "Do you know who that is?"

Sam shook her head. "No, is she someone I should recognize?"

The distinguished-looking gray-haired woman sat sipping tea and gazing at the traffic outside.

"That," Marge said softly, "is Louisa K. Starr, the famous author from Atlanta. She writes terrific novels."

"What kind of novels?"

"Murder mysteries. She has a whole series of them."

"I see," Samantha said. Right away, Sam sensed something sinister about the *famous woman,* but she couldn't be sure what it was.

It was nearly lunchtime when Detective Ronald Johnson stopped by to grab a quick coffee to go before heading back to his office.

"What brings you to our part of town this time?" Sam asked.

"I had to serve a search warrant near here, so I thought a nice hot cup of coffee might get me through lunch. One black coffee, please."

"Sure thing, Detective. Say, we had a famous writer drop by this morning. Louisa K. Starr was here."

"Should I recognize the name?"

"She writes murder mysteries. I thought that would be right up your alley." Sam replied.

"I get enough of that at work. I don't have to read about it."

"I suppose so," Sam chuckled, but quickly became somber. "The thing is, there's something about her that feels evil, but I can't put my finger on it." She paused and brightened. "Anyway, here's your coffee."

Johnson paid for his coffee, then waved and smiled as he left.

Back at the office, he remembered the many times Samantha's *special instincts* had revealed clues to cases he worked on. Could it be happening again?

He called his daughter, who worked at the town library.

"Hi, Dad. What's up? Do you need me to look up something for a case?" Alyssa Johnson asked.

"Maybe," he said. "I wonder if you have any books by Louisa K. Starr?"

"I think we do. Let me check."

After a few moments, she returned to the phone. "I thought we had one. *Toxic Love*. It's in our local author section. She's from here, you know. Should I check it out for you?"

"Why don't you do that," Johnson answered. "I'll stop by your house after work."

That evening, Detective Johnson visited his daughter and picked up the book.

After dinner, he leafed through the pages until something caught his attention. The book's plot involved a woman who poisoned her husband by baking him a pie with the berries of the Pokeweed that sprung up in the family garden.

As he read the chapter, something about the story seemed familiar. It reminded him of a cold case he had worked on years before. It was the case of Marcus Dunne. He continued reading the book and found more similarities, especially the part about Pokeweed. Despite the plant's prevalence in the local area, its potentially toxic qualities remained poorly understood. Several things about the novel differed from the cold case. Dunne lived alone, and there was no evil wife. That, and the fact that Pokeweed poisoning is not usually fatal.

Johnson called his daughter's number.

"Did you read this Toxic Love book?" he asked when Alyssa answered.

"Is that the one about the woman who poisons her husband by baking him a pie with Pokeweed berries from the family garden? "

"That's the one. Something about that story seems familiar. It reminds me of a cold case file I worked on when I started this job. Especially the part about the weed berries. At first they said the death was caused by choking. It wasn't until the medical examiner's report that we learned it was Pokeweed poisoning. That's when it became a cold case."

"Everyone thought it was asthma," his daughter replied.

"The medical examiner's report was never made public. By the time it was released, it was old news. Anyway, thanks for getting me the book. There are too many coincidences. I may have to reopen a cold case on Marcus Dunne," Johnson explained.

"Hey, wasn't he another local author?"

"I need to look into that. That might give me some answers."

They were all part of the local writers' group, " Alyssa replied. "Agnes Toliver still runs that group. You might want to talk to her. I'll text you her email."

The next day at the office, Agnes Toliver answered his email with a phone number.

"Good morning. I wonder if you could tell me something about the history of your group."

"I would be delighted," Toliver responded. "How can I help?"

"I'm curious about someone who may have been in your group a few years back. By chance, was Marcus Dunne a member?"

"Oh, my, yes. It was so sad when he died. Asthma, as I recall."

"Yes, that's what was reported. Did you know him?"

"I have been with this group a long time and I remember him very well."

The Detective dug further: "Does the name Louisa K. Starr mean anything to you?"

"Of course," she replied. "Back then, we knew her as Emily Grace, but everybody else knows her by her pen name, Louisa K. Starr. She grew up here. Did you know that?"

"That's interesting," the detective thought momentarily before asking. "Did she know Marcus Dunne very well?"

"Emily was always very impressed by his writing. He even once referred to her as his muse. She sometimes went to his home and typed out his novels for him. She even cooked for him until his unfortunate death, of course. It wasn't long after that Emily moved to Atlanta. I guess, from there, you might say the rest is history. She's famous, you know."

"So, I've heard," remarked the Detective.

"Are you thinking of becoming a writer?" she asked. "Maybe you could join our group."

"You never know," he answered. "Thank you very much for your time, Miss Toliver. You've been most helpful."

Johnson needed to speak with the *famous author* to clarify some questions.

He made a quick call to the Brown Bean. Marge answered.

"Is that famous author still in town?" he asked.

"Yes, she's been stopping by every morning around ten. She said she was on vacation, staying the week at a condo on the beach. Why do you ask?"

"I picked up her book from the library and thought I might stop by to have a conversation."

"I bet she'll enjoy talking to a fan," Marge responded.

At ten the following day, Johnson found Louisa K. Starr sat at her usual window table with a simple herbal tea. Detective Johnson picked up his black coffee and approached her table to introduce himself.

"Hello, I hope I'm not intruding. I'm a police detective, and I solve mysteries for a living. I recently read one of your books and wanted to meet you."

"Oh," she said, "I'm always glad to meet a fan of my novels! Which one was it?"

"It's *Toxic Love: A Garden of Deceit.* Your stories seem so realistic. Where do you get your inspiration?"

There was a flicker of self-confidence in her eyes. She responded, "I guess I have a vivid imagination. And I do a lot of research."

"This book sounded a lot like a local case we had here a while back."

"Oh, which one was that?" she asked.

"It was the case of a fellow writer you might have known. His name was Marcus Dunne."

"That was a case I studied for the book." The woman tensed briefly. She finally said, "He died of Pokeweed poisoning, like in my book."

"It's amazing that you know that detail," said Johnson.

The author beamed with pride.

"The thing is, I worked that case. Pokeweed poisoning was the actual cause of death, but we never made that part public. Outside of the police, nobody else knew what he died from. But you put it in your book. I'm afraid I'll have to ask you to continue this conversation at the police department to talk about your likely involvement in the death of Marcus Dunne."

At that moment, Starr's expression changed to fear. She then stood and accompanied the Detective to his car.

Upon completion of the investigation, Emily Grace was convicted of the murder of Marcus Dunne.

After the trial, Detective Johnson stopped by the Brown Bean to thank Samantha for once again using her *special abilities* to help him solve the novel investigation. He joined her at the same table where the now infamous author had once spent her mornings.

Sam's reporter-friend Georgiana also stopped by.

"I heard you arrested our famous local author," Georgiana said as she joined the others. "Bring me up to date."

"I brought her in to find out what she knew about a cold case we had, the murder of another author, Marcus Dunne."

"That was before I came here, but I think I heard about it while I was in Atlanta. Didn't he choke to death on a piece of pie or something like that?" Georgiana asked.

"That's what we thought at the time. It turned out to be poisoning. It seems he ingested a lethal amount of Pokeweed berries."

Sam jumped in. "Why would that kill him? Is Pokeweed poisonous?"

"The murderer had to know that in sufficient quantities, it could be fatal, especially if the victim had a serious case of asthma, as Dunne did," Johnson replied.

"Why would anybody want to poison him?" Georgiana asked. "And what does that have to do with Louisa K. Star?"

"That's another interesting detail. It turns out Louisa K. Starr is a pen name. Her real name is Emily Grace, and she used to live here before she moved to Atlanta and became famous. Pretending to be Dunne's muse, she fawned over him. At one point, she baked him a cherry pie. Except it wasn't cherries she put in the pie; it was Pokeweed berries from his own garden, no doubt mixed with a lot of sugar to mask the bitter taste. She had *borrowed* one of his story ideas and didn't want him to find out. With him out of the way, she released his work as her own novel. *Dark Ink, Darker Secrets* was the stolen book that made Emily Grace as famous, as Louisa K. Starr."

"And she confessed?" Sam asked.

Detective Johnson nodded a grim confirmation. "She knew I caught on to her *plot*. She was ready to tell me *the real story*."

"I felt there was something evil about her, but she certainly didn't look the *type*," Samantha admitted.

Georgiana couldn't resist. "Well, you might say she found a *novel* approach to murder."

And Sam chimed in, "And, as they say, the criminal always *returns to the scene of the crime* ... story."

They all enjoyed the laugh.

Chapter Seven

The Intruder

It was a little before eight that morning when Detective Ronald Johnson appeared at the Brown Bean Coffee Shoppe.

"Hey, what brings you by this early?" asked Samantha.

"I'm afraid I'm here on business this time. I need to have a moment with Marge."

"She's in the back. Would you like me to call her out here to the front?"

Johnson raised his head to see Marge working in her small office.

"Is it OK if I speak with her in her office?"

"Sure." Sam turned and waved her hand to get Marge's attention. "Detective Johnson wants to see you."

She met him at the door to the tiny space and beckoned him inside. The detective's expression told her it was not a social visit.

"We may have a problem," he began.

"What's up?" she asked.

"The FTC has had complaints about bogus credit card charges. We started asking the victims where they had recently used their cards for purchases. The Brown Bean kept showing up."

Madge's face turned stern. "They're not accusing us, are they?" she asked.

"No, the bad charges were not made here but at other places. We're trying to figure out if there is a connection."

"How can I help?"

"I need to ask you a few questions. Have you had any new employees?" he asked.

"David is our most recent hire. He works with me and Sam in the morning and goes to classes in the afternoon, but he's been with us for two years now. He is the perfect employee."

"All the same, pay attention to any financial pressures your staff might be facing or uncharacteristic spending."

"Hmm," Marge responded. "How would something like that happen?"

"There could be several ways. An employee might carry a pocket scanning device to collect credit card numbers."

"I'm sure that couldn't happen here. Our customers either swipe or touch their cards at the terminal on the counter. We try not to handle the credit cards."

"That's a good policy. I'll let you know if we find out anything more. In the meantime, I wonder if you could have your network tech call me. I'd like to see if they have noticed anything suspicious."

"I'll ask our tech about it," Marge replied.

With that, he waved goodbye to Samantha and David on his way out. He didn't even stop to order coffee.

Marge was worried that security problems could hurt business.

That afternoon, when Samantha was ready to go home, she noticed a high school student with a laptop at the back of the dining area. The boy was around sixteen, dressed in jeans and a polo shirt.

"Who is that?" she asked Marge.

"That's Joey. He uses our Wi-Fi to do his homework until his mom gets off work. She works in the department store next door. Their apartment building doesn't have internet, so we let him use ours."

"It's nice we can help out a student that way."

Samantha smiled and left for home.

As Sam was clearing tables at the end of work the next day, the student wasn't there, but she noticed a man about her age sitting by the window. She had seen him before. Like the student, he was working on a laptop computer. A backpack leaned against an extra chair, but Sam didn't see it.

She walked by and moved the chair up to the table. As she did, the backpack fell over, spilling the contents, including a device slightly larger than a cell phone. Sam picked it up and gave it to the man at the table. It felt strange in her hand. The man snatched it from her, quickly shoving it back in the bag. With an uneasy smile, he thanked her and returned to what he was doing on the laptop.

Samantha finished cleaning the other tables before heading home to her apartment. She was still trying to decide why she felt something odd when she touched the device that fell out of the backpack. Sometimes, objects have their own psychic energy. It's called psychometry. She decided perhaps that's what it was, but didn't know why.

Late the next morning, Detective Johnson stopped by again. Marge met him at the door and invited him to join her in her office.

"Anything new in your investigation?" Marge asked.

"We're still getting complaints, but the bank is working with their customers to disallow the charges. We may have some clues, though."

"Our IT guy left me a note that he was in last night to check over our network. Did he contact you?"

"That's why I'm here. You may have a digital intruder. From what he told me, someone using your customer's Wi-Fi connection has managed to cross over to the secure network tied to the card reader. The firewall is supposed to stop anyone from crossing over, and the system is encrypted, but whoever it is seems to be getting through. I want to ask your staff if they've noticed anything unusual. You know who I want to talk to first."

"Of course, that would be Samantha." With that, Marge leaned outside the door and gestured to David. "David, can you ask Sam to come to my office?"

David nodded and took over the register from Sam.

Seeing Detective Johnson was still there, she asked, "Is something wrong?"

"Have you noticed any customers acting like they might be doing something illegal? Has your *special radar* picked up anything recently?"

Sam immediately recalled her experience with the customer and the strange device she had picked up from the floor.

"There is one person who comes in several times a week. His backpack spilled, and a little box fell out. He seemed upset when I picked it up to return it to him."

"What did it look like, this little box?"

"It's hard to describe," Sam began. "It looked like a calculator, but I noticed it didn't have any math keys."

"That might be a hacking device." That gave the detective an idea. He asked Marge, "May I have your permission to review the security videos?"

"Of course," Marge answered. "How can that help?"

"Your network tech provided me with a log file of the times when the pay terminal network was accessed. We can match up those times with the timestamp on the surveillance videos. If we find a match with the times our backpack guy was here, that will give me probable cause to see what's in that backpack."

The next day, after a call from Marge, Johnson was back, this time carrying a piece of paper. Marge and Samantha watched as he went directly to the man with the backpack.

"I have a warrant to search that backpack," Johnson said.

The man protested as the detective pulled out the suspected hacking device.

"You are under arrest for suspicion of credit card fraud."

A uniformed officer appeared and took the man into custody. Johnson picked up the backpack and walked to the front counter.

"I guess you found our network intruder," Marge stated.

"We checked the surveillance video and matched it against the times in the network logs, and they matched. We showed the information the data to a judge, and we got an arrest warrant," Detective Johnson responded.

"What was that weird little box I knocked on the floor?" Sam asked.

"As I suspected, it was a Wi-Fi hacking device to record the remote terminal data. We'll leave it to the Feds to figure out all the charges."

Sam had a look of satisfied victory.

"So, I was right. That thing I knocked out of the backpack really was evil, after all."

Detective Johnson nodded agreement.

The following day, Detective Johnson called the coffee shop to report that he had solved the crime. In fact, the little box was a clever hacking device, using AI to break the pay terminal's encryption, collecting and storing credit card information. They then sold the data to a third party.

With a list of federal charges from the FTC, Secret Service, and the FBI, that intruder would not be visiting the Brown Bean again anytime soon.

Chapter Eight

The Mocha Murder Mystery

A tall man walked through the Brown Bean Coffee Shoppe entrance at a steady, deliberate pace, his left hand grasping a guide dog's harness. He wore sunglasses, a brown leather jacket with an Afghanistan War veteran patch on his right shoulder, and khaki pants with side pockets. The dog appeared to be a Labrador/Golden Retriever mix.

The pair stopped when they reached the front counter.

"Good morning. What can I get for you today?" Samantha asked.

"My wife used to make me a special mocha. I was hoping you might have something like it."

"Do you know how she made it?" she asked.

The man smiled as he fondly remembered.

"She told me she would start with a shot of espresso and add some dark chocolate syrup and a touch of cream. Oh, and a sprinkle of cinnamon instead of sugar."

"Then that's how we'll make it for you. Would you like it hot or cold?"

"Hot, please."

"Coming right up," Sam replied, turning to the back counter to gather the ingredients.

When it was ready, she delivered the cup to the counter and looked down at the dog. "Who's your friend?" she asked.

"Oh, that's Sarge, my guide dog. He's all I have left now since Julie died."

"Was Julie your wife?" Sam asked.

"Yes." The old soldier nodded sadly.

"I'm sorry, I'm Jason Thompson." He reached out his right hand.

"Nice to meet you, Mr. Thompson," she said after shaking his hand. "Here's your mocha. I hope it is just like Julie made it for you."

He pulled out his wallet, carefully selecting a five-dollar bill and feeling for a folded corner and placed it on the counter. Sam rang up the sale, put the bill in the drawer, and placed the change in the man's hand.

"May I help you find a table?" she asked.

"That would be nice. Perhaps by the window. I like to feel the sunlight."

Sam motioned for David to take over at the register. Sam guided the man to a window table and pulled up a chair for herself.

"Would you like to tell me about Julie?" she asked.

The man smiled. Sam noticed him touch one eye as he trembled.

"Julie ... When I got back from the war, she was there for me. She was my eyes, you know. Now it's only me and Sarge."

Sam's voice was gentle. "How long has Julie been gone, if I may ask?"

"The funeral was last week."

Sam hesitated before asking, "How did it happen?"

"Somebody came into our apartment and attacked her. A sleeping pill prevented me from hearing the commotion."

The dog moaned. Sam and the dog made eye contact. For a moment, she saw a kitchen stove and a bloody knife. The vision faded, and her mind returned to her conversation with Mr. Thompson.

"Do you want to talk about it?" she asked.

The man paused and took a sip of the mocha. "This is good," he said. "It really is almost like Julie made it."

Sam realized he didn't want to talk about the murder.

"I'll make it exactly that way anytime you come." She tapped her fingers on the table and returned to her duties at the sales counter.

Throughout the rest of the day, Sam kept thinking about the brief vision of a kitchen stove. Where did it come from? Had she connected with the dog? Dogs don't think in words, but some have speculated that they can communicate by projecting images. Was that why he made the soft growling sound to get her attention? As if in answer to an unsaid wish, Detective Johnson appeared at the coffee shop.

"Do you have a minute, or do you need to hurry back to the station?" she asked.

"I'm not in a big hurry, no." He gave Sam a knowing smile. He beckoned to her as he walked toward an open table.

Sam asked, "Do you know anything about a murder case in the neighborhood? A blind man's wife?"

"Julie Thompson," Johnson nodded, almost surprised that Sam knew about the case. "We still don't have any suspects, if that's what you mean. We don't even have the murder weapon. We know it was a knife, but we didn't find one at the crime scene."

Sam blurted out, "Did you look under the kitchen stove?"

"I assure you, the investigators did a thorough job, but the place was messy. I'm almost sure they checked the stove." Johnson paused. "Do you know something more about the case?"

"Mr. Thompson was here this morning. He said his wife used to make his favorite chocolate mocha. He didn't say anything about what happened." Sam paused. Without explaining why, she added, "I just thought it might be good to check under the stove."

Detective Johnson thought for a moment. "I suppose I could stop by to see how Mr. Thompson is doing after his ordeal."

Sam smiled and shook his hand. "I think that would be a good idea."

The detective knocked on the door of Mr. Thompson's apartment.

"Mr. Thompson, it's Detective Johnson. I stopped by to see how you are doing."

He heard the chain on the door, and the door opened.

"How are you getting along?" Johnson asked.

"I'm adjusting. I take my meals over at the VA center now," the old soldier replied.

"Would it be OK if I check the kitchen one more time?" Johnson asked.

Thompson agreed.

The detective stared at the kitchen stove. He then opened the pantry and spotted a yardstick. After pausing for a moment, he took the yardstick and probed the space under the stove. Immediately, he felt a clunk as it struck something solid near the back. He maneuvered the object out and stared in amazement. Covered in dust and blood was the missing murder weapon. Johnson carefully preserved the evidence in a freezer bag he found in a kitchen drawer.

As he was leaving, he said goodbye to Mr. Thompson. The guide dog, Sarge, cocked his head toward the detective and went from sitting at attention to relaxing on the floor.

Back at the police station, Detective Johnson wrote up the evidence report and turned over the bag with the knife to be processed for possible fingerprints.

Sometime later, an officer delivered a report from the fingerprint analysis of the murder weapon.

"You won't have any trouble finding this one," the police officer remarked. "On a hunch, we ran the prints through military records. We came up with a name."

Detective Johnson read from the report: "Corporal James Cortez. Same building as the murder victim. Did we interview this guy?"

"We did, but he claimed not to know anything about the murder in his building."

"This is enough for an arrest, but I want to do a follow up interview. I think there's more to this case."

Reaching the building, Johnson noted the Cortez apartment was on the next floor, directly above the murder scene.

He knocked on the door. The door opened.

"Mr. Cortez, I'm Detective Johnson. I wonder if I can ask you a few more questions for us?"

The man said nothing, but stood aside to let Johnson enter the apartment.

Cortez was a thin man in his late thirties with blonde hair in a crew cut style. He wore a T-shirt and jeans and had not shaved in a few days. He had tattoos covering much of his arms.

The apartment had minimal furniture, and a neatly folded American flag displayed on a small shelf. Johnson glanced at the kitchen and noticed it was almost identical to the Thompson apartment.

"Did you know the Thompsons? Jason Thompson is a fellow veteran."

"No, I didn't know that until I saw it on the news," Cortez said.

When reality sank in, Cortez became emotional, twisting about and groaning, and then he became quiet.

"Sometimes I imagine things, so I keep to myself."

Detective Johnson sensed an opportunity.

"Do you want to tell me what happened that night?"

Cortez stared at the floor as he spoke.

"When I came home, I saw somebody in the kitchen. Didn't even think, just assumed they broke in to steal my food. Grabbed my knife and went at the person like I was back in the field. But it wasn't a damn burglar. Then the dog bit me, and that's when it hit. A dog? In my place? When I figured out it wasn't my apartment, I threw the knife away and ran like hell."

There it was. A confession.

"Are you ready to come with me and sign a statement?" the detective asked.

"I didn't mean to. I didn't know where I was. I just reacted. I didn't mean to kill anybody."

What Cortez didn't know at the time of the crime, in the next room, in a deep sleep, was a fellow veteran sedated to combat a circadian rhythm disorder resulting from his blindness.

The court would reduce the charge to second-degree murder.

Shortly before noon, Detective Ronald Johnson stopped by the Brown Bean.

On seeing Johnson, Sam said, "Georgiana told me you made an arrest in the Thompson case?"

"That's what I came by to tell you. We found the missing murder weapon, got the fingerprints, and a confession."

I'm glad for Mr. Thompson, " Samantha replied, "and it all began with a special mocha."

Chapter Nine

Trouble Brewing

Sandra Smith worked afternoons at the Brown Bean Coffee Shoppe. A single mother of twin teens, both girls, Sandra struggled to make ends meet,

She was at the sales counter when a man about her age stepped up to place an order. He looked to be just under six feet, with a trim, athletic build. His well-groomed dark hair had a touch of gray at the temples, which added a distinguished look.

"Hi, what will you be having today?" Sandra asked, seeming to drink him all in.

He smiled.

"Can you believe I've never been to a coffee shop before? What would you suggest?"

"A lot of people like to go for our latte. We have them in several flavors."

She pointed to the menu board behind her. It listed vanilla, caramel, hazelnut, cinnamon, pumpkin, and about a half-dozen others.

"Why not try our Chocolate Mocha latte?" she suggested. "A lot of people like that."

"OK, I'll try it! By the way, I'm Daryl. And your name is... ?"

"Sandra. I'm Sandra Smith." She tugged at the name badge on her apron.

"I'm pleased to meet you, Sandra."

Their eyes locked for a moment as they both stood in silence.

"Oh! I better get started on your latte!" Sandra said as she turned to the machine on the counter behind the register.

She returned to the sales counter and rang up the sale. Daryl tapped his credit card on the reader. He smiled again as he picked up his order and headed to a table.

Daryl sat drinking his latte while perusing his phone, stopping to watch Sandra as she served other customers. She knew Daryl was watching, but tried not to let him see her notice.

The moment she had a break between customers, Sandra gathered her courage. She took a deep breath to calm her nerves and walked to Daryl's table.

"Is there anything else I can get for you?" she asked.

Daryl put his phone down and leaned back in the chair.

"What do you have planned for Friday night?" he asked.

Sandra didn't know how to react. She couldn't remember the last time she had a proper date. She had to work two jobs to support herself and the twins. It didn't give her much time to think about dating.

She smiled as she scratched the back of her neck, trying to decide what to do.

"What did you have in mind?" she finally asked.

"There's a club a few blocks from here. It's called the Neon Oasis. I've never been there because I never had anybody to go with. The ads make it look nice. It has an Arabian theme, with palm trees, like in the desert."

"And the waitresses wear harem costumes. I thought about working there until I found out about that."

They both giggled.

"So, what do you say?"

"I ... I'll need to make arrangements for my girls."

Sandra was sure that would be an instant turn-off for her new friend.

"Oh, tell me about your girls," Daryl asked. "How old are they?"

"They're twins. Both sixteen, I'm afraid."

"I bet that can be a challenge."

"You have no idea," Sandra answered.

Daryl chuckled. "I'm sure of that!" he said. "You certainly can't leave them alone, can you."

Sandra thought for a minute.

"I have an idea. Let me call my sister. Excuse me for a moment."

She went to the back of the store to get her phone from her purse. Sandra made a quick call to her sister. She was in luck! Her sister agreed to have the twins over for the night.

Sandra almost burst out of the back room as she returned to Daryl's table and sat across from him.

"Guess what! My sister is having the girls over." She pulled a pen from her apron and wrote her address on a napkin, and handed it to Daryl.

"I can be ready by seven. Would that be alright?" Sandra caught herself holding her breath for the answer.

"Sure," Daryl replied, glancing at the address on the napkin as he folded it and put it in his pocket. "See you then!"

Friday afternoon, Sandra met Samantha at the door as Sam was leaving. Sandra was eager to share her news.

"I've got a date tonight!" she told Sam. "Daryl is taking me to the Neon Oasis for drinks and maybe dancing. My sister agreed to watch the twins. It's been a long time since I got to go on an actual date!"

A sudden, a shocking vision struck Samantha. Something about the mention of the Oasis club brought on a premonition of dread. Sam had experienced premonitions before, but this one was different. She was determined to stop Sandra from being at that club that night.

Sandra Smith

Sam frantically blurted out, "You should go to a movie instead."

Sandra had a distressed look on her face. "But we planned to spend the evening at the club…"

"I think you should enjoy a nice movie." Samantha was insistent.

"You clearly don't want us to go to the club, do you! Even if I wanted to see a movie, I don't know if I can talk my date out of going to the club. Neither of us has been there before, but we've heard it can be exciting."

Samantha was becoming desperate. She opened the movie app on her phone and handed it to Sandra.

"You should go to the movies tonight," Sam insisted. "Pick out a great movie, anything you like. My treat, for you and your date!"

Sandra grimaced and reluctantly accepted the phone. She found a movie and pressed the "Buy Ticket" button. Sam copied the QR code and sent it to Sandra's phone.

"I guess I'll just tell my date we have to go because I couldn't turn down free tickets," Sandra said with a shrug.

Samantha smiled with relief. "There you go!" she said, ending the conversation with a thumbs-up gesture.

Later, when Daryl drove up to her apartment, Sandra was waiting outside.

He wore a blue shirt under a tailored blazer and matching pants. He looked sharp!

Sandra had on comfortable jeans and a soft, flowing white blouse. She had a small leather purse with a shoulder strap and carried a light sweater, because theaters tend to be a bit cool.

"I thought you would be dressed up to go to the Oasis," he said.

"Is it alright if we go to the movies instead?" Sandra asked cautiously. "I have free tickets to one I want to see. You don't mind, do you?"

"Sure, no problem, but I'm a little overdressed for the movies, don't you think?"

"You look fine," Sandra said with relief. She didn't want to miss out on this date. "Besides, it's dark in the theater, right? Once we're inside nobody will see us." she reminded him.

"I guess you're right. What time is the movie?"

"We have plenty of time."

"Well, what are we waiting for?" he said as he opened the car door for Sandra.

"You sure you're OK with not going to the club?" she asked.

Daryl responded with a wide grin. "We can go there anytime. We can't waste those movie tickets!"

Sandra felt more relaxed than she had in years. It was going to be a wonderful night.

Meanwhile, it was a busy night at the Neon Oasis. The nightclub was a favorite of the Gen-Y crowd. True to the theme, it featured glowing neon palm trees mixed with Egyptian decorations.

Couples were dancing to techno music played by a DJ wearing a turban. Servers in harem costumes served drinks to couples seated at the tables around the crowded dance floor.

All at once, there was trouble brewing. Two men stood up and began arguing. People around them moved out of the way as the disagreement became more heated. Concern turned to panic when one produced a small pistol. He began waving it in the face of the other man, who grabbed his wrist and pushed the gun away.

The music had stopped by then, and people were rushing for the doors. Then, at the sound of a gunshot, the crowd panicked.

An off-duty policeman hired by the club rushed to confront the two men and defuse the situation. Eventually, the officer restrained the combatants. The DJ had called 9-1-1 as an unlucky bystander lay bleeding on the floor until an ambulance arrived.

Saturday morning at the Brown Bean, Georgiana rushed in.

"Did you hear what happened?" she asked Sam. "There was a fight at the Oasis Club last night. One girl was shot, and a bunch of people were hurt in the panic, trying to get out." Georgiana gestured with her left hand toward the club.

Samantha's expression turned to near shock as she realized her premonition had been confirmed. Her thoughts turned to Sandra and her date. Hopefully, they had enjoyed the movie and avoided the melee at the nightclub.

"Did you hear what I said?" Georgiana asked.

"I'm sorry, yes. How awful. How bad was it?"

"They took the girl who got shot to the hospital, but she's expected to be OK. She wasn't even involved in the fight. Some way to spend an evening, huh!"

"Sandra and her date had been planning on going there last night, but I treated them to a movie instead," Sam said.

"Wow, that was lucky," Georgiana responded.

But Sam wouldn't be able to relax until she was certain Sandra and her date had been at the movies.

That afternoon, Samantha dragged out the task of cleaning the tables before leaving, hoping to catch Sandra when she arrived for her shift.

Sam mentally crossed her fingers as she asked, "How was the movie?"

"It was great!" Sandra replied.

Sam let out a sigh of relief.

"I'm glad you had a good time. You missed some excitement at the club and not the pleasant kind."

"Yeah, I saw the news online this morning. Did you know that was going to happen?" she said suspiciously.

"Let's say I just had a bad feeling about you being there. It was like a vision, you might say."

"Well, my date loved the movie, and I didn't have to explain the real reason we didn't go to the club."

"It's probably better that way," Sam answered with a smile.

"Do you do that a lot? Do you have those feelings? How did you know there would be trouble brewing at the club. I mean, do you scare people like that?"

"Not a lot, but it does happen. I'm learning to accept it."

"Thanks again for the tickets. I still don't know if I believe all this, but I'm glad we weren't at the club."

"Besides," Sandra added, "I really like Daryl. I think he's a *keeper.*"

"Me, too." Sam repeated, "Me, too."

CLOSED

Chapter Ten

The Brown Bean is Closed

Someone had locked the back employee entrance to the Brown Bean Coffee Shoppe from the parking lot. Samantha knocked, but there was no response. She walked around the building to the front. The lights were off, and the front door was locked as well.

The sign in the window said the Brown Bean is closed.

Marge, the manager, was always there before everyone else. Something was not right.

When she heard a buzz, Sam pulled her phone from her purse and scrolled through several missed calls from Georgiana. She touched the button to return the call.

"I've been trying to reach you!" Georgiana said when she answered. "Did you hear what happened to Marge?"

"No! What's going on?"

"I got a tip from a contact at the hospital. Marge got mugged while she was making the day's deposit at the bank. She was seriously hurt. I called the police but all I could get from them was they are trying to get the ATM security video to see what happened."

At that moment, Sam saw David inside, turning on lights and unlocking the door. Still on the phone with Georgiana, she smiled at David and walked inside. David locked the door behind her.

Continuing her phone conversation, Sam asked, "What about Marge? Is she going to be OK? Can I call the hospital?"

"I don't know if the hospital will tell you anything, but you can give it a try. It's too early to reach Detective Johnson, but I'll leave word and see if he can share any details when he gets in."

Sam ended the call with Georgiana.

"How did you find out about Marge?"

"The police called me. Marge put me on the emergency contact list because my apartment is in this building."

"So, what do we do? Can we open?"

David was confident: "We can't get in the safe and there's no cash in the drawer, but we should be able to get by if most people use credit cards. You handle the front and I'll fill the orders. We should be fine, at least for today."

He made a small sign next to the register that read, "*Please use credit cards.*"

"I sure hope Marge is OK. I don't know what we can do if she's out for a long time."

By then, customers were waiting. David nodded as he unlocked the door.

As the day progressed, Samantha and David did their best to keep up.

At noon, Sam called the hospital, but they could or would not tell her about Marge's condition.

David left for school when Sandra arrived for her afternoon shift, and Samantha stayed on to help until closing.

Sam called the hospital again to see if there was any news about Marge's condition. Hearing none, she reached out to Detective Johnson.

"I can't tell you any more than I told Georgiana," the detective told her. "Marge was seriously hurt, but she's awake now, and the doctors are hopeful. We'll know more after a day or so."

"Thanks for filling me in," Sam said. "The hospital wouldn't tell me anything, I guess because I'm not a relative." Changing subjects, Sam continued, "What about your investigation? Can you find out who did it?"

"We checked the surveillance video from the ATM, but it was dark. We don't have a clear picture of the attacker. Maybe you can stop by and take a look. It might be somebody you've seen at the coffee shop. He certainly seemed to know Marge's routine."

At the police station, after the shop closed that afternoon, Detective Johnson showed her the video.

"I think I've seen that guy. Can you stop the video and roll it back? There! He has his hand around her neck. Is that a snake? A tattoo of a snake? I'm almost sure I've seen that tattoo before."

"There could be many people with that same tattoo, but it might give us something to go on. Be careful! Let me do the investigating."

He continued, "Thanks for coming by. I'll let you know if we find anything."

Detective Johnson called Sam the following day at the Brown Bean.

"I thought you would want to know. We checked the dumpster near the bank and found an empty bank bag. The serial number matches the Brown Bean. It's in the lab now. There might be prints we can use for evidence. We need to find that guy with a snake tattoo."

Samantha stopped by the hospital for an afternoon visit. Marge's condition had improved, and she was eager to return to work. She seemed more concerned about that than her recovery. Marge was happy to see Samantha.

"You're awake!"

"Yeah, the police told me what happened. I don't remember much. That guy must have hit me pretty hard. I'm usually more careful and aware of my surroundings."

Sam reached out and touched Marge lightly, seeking to reassure her. As she did, she had a vision of a street sign, or at least a fragment of one. She didn't recognize the street name, but she made a quick mental note of what she saw. The vision faded. It had only lasted a few seconds.

A doctor stopped by the room and checked Marge's chart.

"Good evening," he said. "Based on your chart, you could go home tomorrow if your test results are normal."

That was news Marge wanted to hear. Sam told Marge that many customers had been asking about her and that she and David were sharing duties in her absence. They talked until visiting hours were over, and Sam left for home.

In her mind, Samantha kept going over the vision of the letters *"STLE"*. It was late, but she wandered through several side streets before stopping at a traffic light. She noticed the street sign: *Newcastle Street.* It matched the letters she saw in her vision. While the light was still red, she each way. In one direction, she saw a seedy tavern. Detective Johnson had warned her to let him do the investigating, so when the light turned green, she headed for home.

On her break the next day, Samantha called Detective Johnson.

"How's the investigation coming?" she asked.

"So far, not much. The partial fingerprints we got from the bank bag only narrowed us down to about a dozen people, I'm afraid."

"I could have something to add."

"Please don't tell me you've been doing your own investigating. I told..." Sam cut him off.

"No, of course not, but I think I know where you could look for our snake tattoo guy. There's a tavern on North Newcastle Street."

"Where did you get the information?" he asked.

"Let's just say it just popped into my head."

By now, Johnson had come to accept Samantha's "special" perceptions. They had already paid off for him several times.

"Let me see what I can find. We sure don't have much to go on so far. I might have one of my undercover guys check it out to see if our snake tattoo guy shows up."

As it would happen, on the first night, the undercover officer spotted a man with a snake tattoo on his arm. The officer waited until the man left the bar and hurried to where he had been drinking a beer. He jammed his fist inside the beer mug, careful not to touch the handle or the sides, and slipped it under his coat. With any luck, the mug could supply the fingerprints needed to solve the case. If the bartender saw what was happening, he didn't let on, and the officer made his way out the door with the mug. In his car, the officer placed the mug in an evidence bag.

The mug went to the fingerprint lab. In a couple of days, they could have the results.

The fingerprint database returned a match for a Vincent Marlow. Now, they only needed to capture him. Police set up a stakeout. At last, they saw their suspect arriving. Officers moved in as he approached the tavern entrance. Police took him into custody without incident.

The police charged Marlowe with the ATM mugging and robbery.

Detective Johnson called Samantha with the news. Once again, his "secret weapon" had helped solve another case.

Later, when Marge was back at work at the Brown Bean. She gestured, inviting Samantha to come to her office.

At the door, Sam greeted her with a warm "Welcome back."

"Thank you. This experience has taught me a lesson. This coffee shop depends on me too much. I need a backup. What do you think?"

The implication was that Samantha was who she had in mind. Sam thought for a moment.

"David is studying business management in college. We worked as a team while you were in the hospital. I think he would be a good choice, and it would give him some good real-world experience."

Marge tilted her head and nodded. "I was thinking of you, but you're right, of course."

Samantha smiled and said, "I'll let David know you want to see him."

Chapter Eleven

A Bitter Scoop

One morning, Samantha Wilson was returning to the front counter after retrieving a stack of latte cups from the storeroom. David Miller was ringing up a sale at the register.

"Marge would like to speak to you in the office when you get a minute."

David nodded and walked to the office in the back of the stockroom.

"Good morning, Marge. You asked to see me?" he said.

"You're taking college courses. As I recall, you're studying business management, right?"

"That's right. I hope to operate a business one day."

"Would you like an opportunity for some practical experience?" Marge asked.

"I sure would!" David tried not to sound too eager.

The offer made sense. Marge worked long hours. She always opened the shop in the morning and was there for closing.

"Let's see how you do as assistant manager. You and Samantha can handle mornings, and I'll come in and work with Sandra in the afternoon. How does that sound?"

David did not hesitate. "I'm pleased to accept the opportunity."

"Then it's settled. Let's go over some things. I'll still handle scheduling, but you'll need to know about the reports and managing the cash register."

David wondered how Samantha would take the news. She had been working at the shop longer than he had. However, as he returned to the front counter, her knowing smile told him she was happy for him.

As time went on, David was eager to accept his extra responsibilities. He recognized business traffic was strong in the morning, but by afternoon, the line of customers dwindled to none.

David was eager to apply his college training to his new position. He approached Marge with some ideas.

"I've been thinking about ways to increase business, particularly in the afternoon."

"You're right. That's been a problem. I thought about expanding the menu, but we don't have the space for a kitchen. I once considered *coffee and dessert* in the evenings, but the staff scheduling wouldn't work out. When I mentioned adding wine to the menu, the owner, Mr. Davis, was dead set against it, so that was that."

David was confident he had done his homework.

"I thought we should consider offering ice cream. It would only need some space for a freezer case next to the register, and we might even attract some of the school kids we see walking by."

Marge considered the suggestion for a moment and then smiled.

"I'll mention the idea to Mr. Davis, and if he has no objections, I'll let you work out the details."

David was ready. He reached into his pocket and unfolded a sheet of paper with a list of ice cream suppliers and sources for a freezer case.

When Marge got the owner's approval the next day, David went to work.

A salesman stopped by to speak with David. They talked for a time in the office. The ice cream supplier representative brought along a small cooler with samples of ice cream. David expressed his surprise at how remarkably smooth the ice cream sample tasted.

"I'll let you know the manager's decision, but I'm confident she will approve of your offer," he said. The two shook hands as the salesman left.

David made his presentation to Marge.

"The supplier can provide us with the ice cream, and I found a source for the freezer display case," David said as he handed her the proposed agreement. "We can get the cones, cups, and spoons from our regular supplier."

Marge looked over the paperwork and gave her approval. David called and placed the first order and had a local print shop design window posters announcing the new product. He ordered ice cream cups with the Brown Bean Coffee Shoppe logo.

A few days later, a truck arrived to install the freezer display case, and later, another truck delivered the ice-cream. The Brown Bean was ready to sell ice-cream.

Sure enough, the idea quickly resulted in an increase in business, not only in the afternoon. Customers stood in line for ice-cream throughout the day.

While Samantha didn't want to spoil David's success, she had a negative premonition. She couldn't decide what it was. But the moment she touched the ice-cream bucket, she saw shadowy figures clutching their stomachs. As soon as she drew back her hand, the vision melted away.

She hesitated before telling David. She was worried about how he would react, or if he would believe her.

"I had a vision, a bad premonition," she whispered, her voice trembling.

David frowned.

"Sam, we can't make business decisions based on ... visions."

"But we can't ignore them either," Samantha insisted, her voice more robust now. "This isn't just a feeling. It's a warning. There's something wrong with this ice cream," she told him. "We can't keep serving it to customers."

David felt both concern and annoyance, and he tried to shake off the unease creeping up his spine.

"I think you're overreacting," David snapped, his frustration becoming obvious. "The health department would not let something careless slip through. I've done my research, and everything checks out. Maybe you're just stressed."

Samantha was adamant. "I'm telling you, David, something is not right. I trust my instincts."

David shook his head, exasperated. "Not everything can be solved with a hunch, Sam. This is a business; we need to be practical, not paranoid."

Samantha inspected the packaging for the list of ingredients and found nothing to be concerned about. And yet, the negative sensation remained.

"There's something they're not telling us," she insisted.

Still, David dismissed her concerns.

At first, the customers received the ice cream well, but soon, a few began complaining about what might have been allergic reactions.

Could it be that Samantha was right?

Georgiana stopped by for her usual latte and noticed the addition of the new ice cream display case.

"We've had some calls at the TV station from people complaining about their reactions after eating ice cream," she said as she peered at the new freezer case next to the sales counter. "Things like nausea and stomach cramps, mostly."

David overheard the conversation.

"We've had very few customer complaints," he replied. "Nothing serious. Probably just allergies."

"Just the same, there has been enough local concern that I'm working on a special report on all the places that sell ice cream and the ice cream suppliers in the area. I'm collecting samples, and the lab at the university in Athens has agreed to run some tests. Would you mind letting me have a sample for the test?"

David reluctantly agreed. "I suppose we can't take chances. If our customers are getting sick, that could mean serious problems for the Brown Bean, and Marge would hold me responsible."

Georgiana went to her news truck parked outside and returned with a portable cooler. She also brought a plastic lab container, which she labeled "Brown Bean," and the date. She then put on disposable gloves and removed a small scoop from a sealed plastic bag. Georgiana next collected a small sample of vanilla ice cream and placed it in the sample container. She put the sample in the cooler with some other samples she had collected earlier in the day. Dry ice in the cooler would ensure the sample would remain frozen. She also took a picture of the ingredients label with her phone camera and noted the supplier's name.

"I'll let you know what I find and when we plan to broadcast my report," she said as she left with the cooler.

Georgiana took the samples to the food testing laboratory at the university in Athens.

After a few days, they had the results.

The university conducted the tests using a Gas Chromatography-Mass spectrometer. There was nothing dangerous in any of the samples, but they found small traces of palm oil in several samples, including one from the Brown Bean. Palm oil is a common ingredient in many brands of ice cream, and it can be an attractive option for ice cream manufacturers as a substitute for dairy fats or cocoa butter. The benefit is that it can extend the shelf-life of ice cream, prevent the formation of ice crystals and slows melting when exposed to room temperature. And it's cheaper than the alternatives.

It also can improve the texture, which would account for the smooth taste David had noticed in the sample. However, while still within health department limits, the manufacturer of that particular brand used slightly more than the other brands.

The lab report suggested the amount of palm oil might be the answer to the puzzle.

Georgiana's special TV report, "Bitter Scoop," assured local viewers that the amount of palm oil in the samples was safe, although local restaurants and others planned to switch suppliers.

Soon, the Brown Bean received a new shipment of ice cream. The cost was a little more, and the ice cream was not as smooth tasting as the other brand, but customer complaints disappeared immediately.

Samantha noticed the different brand on the ice cream tubs.

"I see you made the switch," Sam remarked to David, trying not to sound like an *I told you so*. "That was a good executive decision," Sam said, congratulating David. "You're right for this job."

"I was worried you might be jealous of my promotion."

Samantha smiled. "Don't be silly. This is what you're going to school for."

David's clear relief showed any fears he may have had about the growing tension between them were gone.

When Marge came in later that day, she also complimented David.

"You made a good call with the ice cream idea. And you handled the problem with the supplier well. Looks like I made the right decision promoting you to assistant manager."

Marge even hinted that they might need to add an extra employee and possibly extend closing hours into the evening. Later closing time would mean more hours for Sandra, and she could certainly use the extra money.

Samantha couldn't help but smile. Her unique gift had once again unraveled a perplexing situation, leading to good things for everyone involved.

Chapter Twelve

Black Gold

When Samantha and David opened up in the morning, they found a note from Marge taped to the register. The note said that a shipment of coffee beans had been delivered to the stockroom. David had ordered from a local importer so the Brown Bean could provide their customers with the freshest ground coffee possible. He set up the register for the new day, while Samantha wandered into the stockroom to check out the delivery.

She entered the storage area and saw two bags on the floor marked "Café de Oro Importers." Sam gasped as a translucent figure suddenly materialized, seemingly from behind the coffee bags. A gaunt man in tattered work clothes reached out toward her. Sam quickly backed away, reached for the switch, and flicked on the light.

The ghost disappeared.

Shaken, Sam returned to the front counter and busied herself with minor tasks, her mind wrestling with what she had just seen or imagined.

Later in the day, Georgiana arrived, and Samantha shared her strange encounter.

"The ghost of a farmworker, perhaps? But what was a ghost doing in a coffee bean bag?" Georgiana sipped on her latte, her brow furrowing.

"I wouldn't say he was in the coffee bag, but maybe his spirit was somehow connected to it. The bag said it came from Colombia."

Georgiana was thoughtful for a moment. "But why would he try to communicate with you?"

"That's what I'm trying to figure out," Samantha replied.

"Do you think we should ask Detective Johnson?" Georgiana asked.

"What can he do about it?" Sam asked. "Whatever happened to this person, it was probably in South America."

"You're right. He probably can't help. I wonder who would listen to us? And what would we tell them? We saw a ghost in a coffee bag?"

After Georgiana left, Sam returned to the stockroom, turned out the light, and waited. Slowly, the apparition appeared once more.

"Who are you?" she asked. She listened and thought she heard a whisper.

"Soy Carlos Mendoza," the voice said. "¡Ayúdanos! "

It then faded away, leaving Samantha bewildered and wondering what she should do. She called Georgiana's number, but the call went to voice-mail.

When Georgiana returned the call, Sam shared the ghost's name and what she thought she heard it say.

"I think *ayudanos* means help us," Georgiana suggested. "Let's run this by Detective Johnson. It's way out of his jurisdiction, but I still want to find out what he thinks about all this. Maybe we won't mention the ghost."

Later that day, Georgiana reached Detective Ronald Johnson at his office.

"Do you know anyone with connections to Colombia?" she asked. "Specifically, the coffee trade?"

"How so?"

Georgiana thought about how to answer.

"It's about a likely victim of something, maybe murder ... in Colombia. The name is Carlos Mendoza. It has some connection with a local coffee importer, Cafe de Oro."

"I won't ask about your source, but the connection to coffee, I can probably guess. Let me see what I can do."

Georgiana could almost hear the smirk on his face as he said it. At least he wasn't dismissing the question out of hand.

A quick online check on slave labor and coffee plantations by the detective revealed a surprising amount of information. The Brazilian government rescued eighteen workers in slave-like conditions in a raid of one of the most extensive coffee plantations. Further research revealed similar conditions in neighboring Colombia, which is the third largest coffee exporter behind Vietnam and Brazil.

Johnson sent a text message to Marco Rossi, an old friend at Interpol, the agency that primarily facilitates communication and cooperation between law enforcement agencies of different countries.

A few minutes later, his phone buzzed.

"Hey, Ron, I got your text. What's this about an unofficial inquiry?"

Ronald sighed. "Thanks for the call, Marco. I'm checking out a tip involving a possible crime victim connected to a coffee plantation in Colombia."

"Of course, I can't officially help you with this, but you might want to ask Customs and Border Patrol about an importer in your area, named Café de Oro. That's all I can tell you, and don't tell them where you heard it."

There was that name again: Café de Oro.

Johnson glanced at his watch. It was getting late in the day. He drummed his fingers nervously on his desk before dialing the number of another old friend from the police academy. Agent Mike Sanders was with the Georgia office of Customs and Border Protection. After two rings, a familiar voice answered.

"Sanders here."

"Mike. It's Ron Johnson. Got a minute?"

"Hey, Ron, long time, man. What's up?"

Johnson lowered his voice and glanced at the closed door of his office.

"I need to ask you something off the record. I heard through the grapevine that you were looking into a local coffee importer, Cafe de Oro."

There was a pause on the line. "Okay, shoot. But let's keep it unofficial."

"Right. What can you tell me about their operations in Colombia? I'm working on a tip about one of the plantations, and a guy named Carlos Mendoza who might be a victim of something."

Sanders sighed. "Damn, Ron. I can't give you specifics, but I will say this – that importer has had our attention for a while now. There have been serious ... rumors, let's say, about their labor practices."

"Any way you could pass that name by the authorities in Colombia?"

"Officially, no. Unofficially, let me see what I can do. The South American coffee trade is lucrative, at least for the two giant companies that control half the world market. Those on top sometimes refer to coffee as black gold. While global consumption of coffee has doubled in the last twenty years, workers may take home very little, often working under the threat of violence."

"I appreciate it, Mike. See what you can find. I owe you one."

Unknown to Detective Johnson, instigated by his inquiry, the wheels started turning in Colombia. Unmarked trucks moved along a muddy access road. Inside were members of Colombia's National Police anti-trafficking unit. With half a million small coffee farms in Colombia, this one was one of the most remote.

When the team reached the main gate, floodlights came on and shouts echoed across the plantation. The exchange of gunfire filled the morning mist with the acrid smell of gunpowder. National officers took positions while shadowy fig-

ures darted between buildings on the plantation grounds.

Officers took aim at a sniper on a nearby rooftop. The police moved in, and the plantation's resistance crumbled. Some of the armed guards threw down their weapons. They raised their hands behind their heads and the officers took them into custody.

Within minutes, the click of handcuffs replaced the sound of gunfire. Additional vehicles arrived to haul away the prisoners.

Farmworkers soon emerged from tiny shelters. In all, eighteen workers were rescued. All showed signs of malnutrition and mistreatment. Their faces displayed a mix of fear, confusion, and gratitude for their rescue.

A later investigation revealed the recent death of one worker, Carlos Mendoza, at the hands of the plantation operators while trying to escape.

Word got back to Johnson's contact at Customs and Border Patrol, and Johnson answered his friend's call.

"Hey, Ron," Sanders said. "I just got a report on that import company. Colombian officials tracked down the name you gave me. They uncovered a slave labor operation. The plantation was the principal supplier for Café de Oro, so we shut down their import operations here. I appreciate the tip."

"I'm glad it worked out, Mike, and thanks for the information. I have some people here who will be glad to hear it."

It was late, but Johnson made a call to Georgiana.

"You might be interested to learn that Customs and Border Patrol shut down the import operations of Cafe de Oro. It turns out they were connected to a slave labor operation on a coffee plantation in Colombia."

Georgiana could not hide her relief and joy. "I'm glad it all worked out."

"I'm sure Samantha has to be involved in this some way, so you can let her know what happened. The bad part is, they'll probably have to find a new supplier."

Georgiana could be heard chuckling. "I'm sure that won't be a problem. Thank you, Detective. It's always nice to hear from you."

After hearing Georgiana's news, Samantha walked into the storeroom. She flicked off the light and called out.

"Carlos, if you're here, we heard you. They've been stopped."

There was no response from the ghost, but somehow Samantha knew her message got through.

Chapter Thirteen

Spooking a Ghost

'T was just after the noon hour on Halloween eve, and all through the Brown Bean Coffee Shoppe, Samantha, and Marge were finishing the last of the Halloween decorations.

Strands of fake spider webs clung to the corners of the menu board above the front counter. The tables had holiday centerpieces featuring plastic pumpkins and fall leaves. Napkin holders held bright orange napkins. Small witches rode magical broomsticks across the front windows. A small signboard listed seasonal beverages, including Ghostly White Chocolate, witch's Brew Smoothie, Monster Cookies, and, of course, the obligatory Pumpkin Spice Latte.

Marge wore a witch's hat and a black cape while Samantha dressed up as a lady pirate, complete with a three-cornered hat and a patch over one eye.

Sandra arrived for work a little early as Samantha and Marge were finishing the decorations.

"You didn't leave anything for me to do," Sandra feigned a protest as she stood behind the counter, taking it all in. "It all looks really nice!"

Everyone who dressed up in a costume received a free ice cream cone or pastry with their coffee order. Many of the regular customers joined in the spirit of the occasion.

A tall, slender woman entered, dressed as a classic vampire. Her long black gown flowed to the floor, with a high collar framing her pale face.

Dark red lipstick accentuated her features, while her long dark hair cascaded down her back, flowing over a cape that billowed as she walked.

Approaching the counter, she spoke in a smooth and theatrical voice, "I'll have a blood orange latte, please, and make it extra spooky!"

Sandra smiled, "And how are you today, Miss Walker, "recognizing the familiar voice of the local English teacher. "Try not to bite anyone while I get that for you."

Moments later, a woman walked in wearing a costume that included a brown tunic with orange accents, complete with a foam-like headpiece intended to look like whipped cream with just a sprinkle of cinnamon.

Sandra laughed. "How about a pumpkin spice latte to match your costume?"

"It's Alice," the woman said, "and yes, please."

"Yes, I know," Sandra said smugly, looking back at the counter as she turned the handle of the espresso machine to fill the cup. She adds all the ingredients. When it was done, she delivered the drink to the counter and rang up the sale.

A mother and daughter arrived. Susan, a mother in her thirties, dressed as a classic witch, complete with a flowing black dress and a pointed black hat. Her makeup featured a touch of green face paint. Mia, her six-year-old daughter, had her own witch costume. Mia's dress was a mix of black and purple, topped with a miniature witches hat as she carried a small cauldron-shaped candy bucket already containing a few wrapped candies. Marge reached into a jar on the counter and dropped a small bag of candy pumpkins into her bucket.

"Mom, can we get the ghost cookies?" Mia asked, her eyes wide with anticipation as she gazed into the display in the glass case on the counter.

Meanwhile, a man at a corner table waved to each customer as they arrived. His elaborate steampunk costume included a brown leather vest over a gleaming white shirt, with a pair of goggles perched on his forehead.

He had a pocket watch dangling from his vest and he leaned a cane with intricate carvings against the table.

The bell on the door rang as a tall figure in a flowing white sheet entered. The classic ghost costume included cut-outs for eyeholes.

Sandra spoke to the newcomer in a friendly but firm tone.

"Welcome to the Brown Bean. I'm sorry, but we have a strict policy against full face covers."

The ghost did not respond, and instead moved closer to the counter

Marge, who had been arranging the pastries, moved beside Sandra, her voice calm but authoritative.

"We need to see your face, for security reasons."

Customers took notice of what was happening. Samantha, amid arranging table decorations, paused as her focus shifted to the activity at the register.

The ghost remained silent for a moment and then spoke in a low and muffled voice.

"I don't think so."

In a swift motion, the figure reached a white gloved hand into the folds of the costume and pulled out a handgun. Pointing it at Sandra and Marge, he announced, "This is a robbery. You will please open the cash register and stand away."

A collective gasp rippled through the café. The steampunk adventurer half-rose from his seat but froze when the ghost swung the gun in his direction.

Marge and Sandra slowly raised their hands.

"Okay, let's stay calm," she said as she reached toward the register. "I'm going to unlock the drawer."

"Do it!" the ghost ordered, waving the gun.

Marge carefully turned the key, releasing the cash drawer, and it opened.

"Both of you get back," the ghost ordered as he slipped behind the counter.

Samantha's eyes squinted as she focused all her concentration on the open cash drawer. Suddenly, to her amazement, the cash drawer began moving, seemingly on its own. It slowly slid shut.

Startled, the ghost looked around the room in confusion.

"Hey, open it back up," he demanded.

Bewildered, Marge stepped forward hesitantly. As she reached for the drawer, it slid open again of its own accord.

Sandra's eyes widened as she glanced at Samantha. Sam touched a finger to her lips.

The ghost, clearly unnerved, reached for the cash. Just as his hand was about to touch the money, the drawer slammed shut with a loud bang.

"What's going on?" the ghost demanded, his voice rising in panic. He waved the gun wildly. "Is this some kind of trick?"

Samantha, worried someone might be hurt, concentrated harder, and the drawer rattled and vibrated. The ghost stumbled backward and lowered the gun.

"This place is haunted!" he cried out as he turned and ran, the white sheet billowing behind him.

For a moment, everyone in the Brown Bean Coffee Shoppe remained in stunned silence. Then a burst of relieved laughter and excited chatter broke out.

The vampire lady fanned herself dramatically with her cape.

"Well, that was more excitement than I bargained for with my latte!"

A man in a skeleton costume approached the counter. "That was amazing! How did you make the drawer move like that?"

Marge, thinking quickly, forced a smile. "We installed a remote control. For, uh, security purposes."

"Wow! That's quite a trick! You sure spooked that ghost, didn't you. You folks have a safe Halloween now!"

With that, he waved goodbye and left the shop.

As the excitement died down, customers returned to their conversations. Samantha continued wiping tables. Sandra caught her eye, and Sam responded with a sly grin. Sandra's face revealed a dawning realization.

Marge recounted some things she had been observing about Sam.

She approached Samantha's table and spoke in a hushed tone. "Sam, was that ... you?"

Sam glanced around to be sure no one was listening, then nodded slightly.

"I'm not exactly sure how, but ... I just wanted the drawer to move, and it did."

Marge shook her head with a broadening smile. "No!"

Samantha slowly nodded.

Sandra approached to see what they were talking about.

"Don't you suppose we should tell Detective Johnson what happened?"

Marge pursed her lips and tilted her head. "No, I don't think we need to do that. After all, there was no robbery, was there?"

Sandra looked at Samantha and back at Marge.

"Nothing happened, did it!"

Georgiana did not agree. "There was an attempted robbery. Somebody could have been hurt. We need to tell the police."

"I guess you're right," Marge agreed.

With that, Samantha handed Marge the cloth she had been using to wipe down tables, raised her eye patch, and said, "Then, I guess it's time for me to get my purse and go home."

Just another day at the Brown Bean Coffee Shoppe!

Chapter Fourteen

A Brewed Awakening

Channel 27's morning show was playing on the TV at the Brown Bean. David served customer orders, but Samantha's attention focused on the featured interview. The host of *Georgia Dawn*, Katie Collins, was interviewing author Marcus Blackwell about his new book, *Hidden Mind: Unveiling Psychic Secrets*.

"Welcome to Channel 27 Georgia Dawn," Katie greeted her guest. "What inspired you to write this book and delve into the world of psychic phenomena?"

"Thanks for inviting me to speak with you. My inspiration came from my experience investigating unexplained phenomena. I realized how little we truly understand about human consciousness."

"In your book, you talk about psychic abilities as being something many of us might possess. How can the average person tap into these abilities?" Katie asked.

Blackwell thought for a moment before responding. "Everyone has experienced moments of intuition. Meditating can help people become more aware of their abilities."

"I'm sure there is no shortage of skeptics who believe it's all coincidences or a trick of the mind. How do you respond?"

"Skepticism is healthy, but we must remain open to possibilities. I present well-documented cases in my book, cases that challenge conventional explanations. I encourage my readers to examine the evidence and draw their own conclusions."

Katie asked, "Can you share a surprising or compelling case you encountered in your research?"

"One case involved a woman who accurately described a crime scene miles away. She provided details that led police to solving the case. It's all in my book in chapter seven."

The case was like Sam's experience. The TV sound was off, and the interview appeared in subtitles on the screen.

David was not aware of Sam's secret, and she was relieved his attention was on preparing customer orders and not on the TV.

The television interview continued.

"What might you say to someone who has had a paranormal experience?" Katie asked her guest.

"I would say, you're not alone. Many people have paranormal experiences, but are afraid to share them with others, in fear of drawing attention or ridicule."

"What do you hope your readers will take away from reading your book, even if they don't believe in psychic phenomena?"

The author responded, "My book encourages open-mindedness and critical thinking, whether the reader believes in psychic abilities. It's an invitation to explore the boundaries of what we think is possible."

With that, the host thanked the author for the interview and the program ended.

Just before noon, it happened. Sam recognized the face when a man in a business suit stepped up to the order counter. What were the odds he would decide to visit this part of town? However, the man's attention appeared to be focused on David, preparing the orders behind the counter.

As David brought the Cappuccino to the order counter, he directed a question to David.

"I believe I can sense some psychic energy in this cafe. Have you ever had any paranormal experiences?"

Samantha's mind raced. Why would he ask David that question?

David replied, "No, I guess not. There have been times when I've wondered about it, though."

The man then reached into a coat pocket and produced a business card. "I wrote a book about it. Perhaps you saw the interview on the local TV channel this morning. Here's my card."

David glanced briefly at the card, paused for a moment, and smiled.

"No, I was working all morning. Maybe I'll check it out," he replied as he slipped the card into his shirt pocket and went back to his tasks behind the counter.

After the man left, and they weren't busy, David turned to Samantha.

"What do you think about what that man said about paranormal things? Are they real?"

Samantha wasn't sure how to answer. Finally, she shrugged and tried to look uninterested as she replied, "You never know, do you?"

David had not witnessed the event with the ghost, so she was hoping it could end there.

Unfortunately...

Just before noon, Mr. Blackwell was back.

Again, his attention is on David.

"Are you sure you haven't experienced anything out of the normal?" he questioned David. "I can't help but feel there is something paranormal about this coffee shop."

It was almost time for David to leave for class and the man was becoming an annoyance when Samantha came to his rescue.

"Perhaps you are sensing one of our artifacts," she said, gesturing to the various antique coffee artifacts displayed around the room.

The author turned his head to consider the possibilities. Samantha concentrated her energy on a particular coffee pot.

Marcus Blackwell squinted his eyes as the old pot briefly exhibited a soft glow, and he cautiously walked toward it. The glow was gone as quickly as it had appeared.

The activity had escaped the attention of everyone in the shop except for Samantha, the author, Blackwell, and David.

David turned his head as if to study what he was seeing.

Meanwhile, Blackwell reaches out and touches the old pot. Perhaps he was expecting a lightning bolt to shoot out of it, but nothing happened. He stepped back, touching his hand to his face, as if deciding what to make of the situation. Finally, he returned to the order counter and apologized to David.

"I'm sorry if I made you feel uncomfortable," he said, apologizing to David. "For a moment I thought I sensed something, but it was probably my imagination."

With that, Blackwell left.

David said nothing until Madge came to take over the sales counter. As usual, Samantha was tidying up the tables, getting ready to leave for the day. David approached her and stood for a moment before speaking.

"What do you think of what that man said?" David asked.

Samantha tried to feign ignorance. "About what?"

"About, you know, strange experiences."

"What do you think," Sam asked, strategically.

"I feel as though I am just awakening to something. Now that I think about it, there could have been some strange things that have happened here at the coffee shop." He leaned forward and looked into Samantha's eyes as he spoke.

From the counter, Marge was observing the conversation and tried to think of a way to rescue Samantha.

Finally, she spoke up, "Isn't it about time for you to go to your class?"

The look of relief on Samantha's face was unmistakable. Her secret was safe. For now.

David turned his head with a smile. It's possible he knew the answer, but he said nothing as he waved goodbye to Marge and Sam and headed to his classes.

Samantha smiled at Marge with unspoken appreciation as she took off her apron and retrieved her purse before leaving for home.

Chapter Fifteen

Lost and Found

On the way home after a long day at the end of a busy week, Samantha stopped off to stock up on a few things at the grocery store. Once home at her apartment, she took a quick shower and plopped onto the couch with a book.

Hours later, she was thinking about what she might fix for dinner when her phone rang. She glanced at the name as she reached for her phone. What would Georgiana be calling about at six in the evening? Shouldn't she be working?

"Hey, what's up?" Sam answered.

"The station is running a special program, so we didn't have a six o'clock report. Since I'm off early, I thought we could have a girl's night out. What do you think?"

"That sounds like a nice idea. What do you have in mind? A movie? A club?" Sam asked.

"I have something more interesting in mind. I just found out there's a cold case and unsolved crimes tour in town at the police museum. It starts at eight."

"Police museum? I didn't know there even was such a thing. That would be something different."

"How about I pick you up in a half hour? We can grab something to eat on the way."

Right on time, Georgiana pulled up outside Samantha's apartment in her red Toyota Celica. Sam had been watching from a window and came outside.

Grabbing a quick meal at a taco place on the way, they pulled into a parking space in front of a small warehouse building. Georgiana had purchased the tickets online and showed the QR code at the tour desk. They passed through a set of heavy doors, past a mannequin of a hunter holding a bloody ax, to join the small group already there.

Samantha scanned the variety of exhibits. Many consisted of photos on poster boards with strings attached to colored pins, while others displayed various pieces of evidence, like knives and old pistols, either actual or replicas.

A distinguished-looking gentleman dressed in an old-fashioned police uniform and cap gazed briefly at his pocket watch.

"Good evening," he said. "Welcome to our crime and unsolved cases tour."

He continued, "According to the data from Operation Cold Case, there have been more than eleven thousand unsolved homicide crimes in the state since 1980. Tonight, we will be exploring some of the most interesting cases."

"We begin with of a man found dead near the iconic fountain in Forsyth Park. He was a local Civil War historian, Dr. Harold Finch. It was a bizarre case indeed. Why he was at the park and who he might have encountered was never determined."

"In what way was it strange," one guest asked.

"His body was propped up on a park bench, pierced by a sword dating back to the Civil War days. Witnesses reported seeing someone wearing a Civil War uniform, a Yankee uniform, in fact, but they thought it was part of some event in the park. But there was no event scheduled."

"I guess they never found out who did it," a plump woman in her sixties remarked.

"That's right. The mystery soldier was never found, and the murder was never solved."

The tour guide then narrated the details of several other exhibits in the room, complete with various evidence simulations, draped with yellow crime scene tape.

"This last case is more recent," the guide explained. The display included a photograph on the wall and a journal resting on a table.

"Dr. Ming Zhang was a professor of forensic science here at the police academy. One day, he was there, and the next day, there was no sign of him. He didn't return to his apartment and was never seen again."

Someone in the group asked, "What about his phone?"

"His phone was left on the desk in his office, but he was known to be forgetful. The police contacted his family, but they haven't heard from him in over a year."

While the question distracted the group, Samantha gazed at the professor's photo. Then, on impulse, she discretely reached through the ropes to briefly touch the journal and quickly pulled back her hand.

She whispered to Georgiana, "That professor is here."

Georgiana had a startled look. "What are you talking about?" she whispered back as she glanced around the room.

"I mean, Dr. Zhang is still around."

Georgiana turned to notice the tour guide staring in their direction, his irritation on his face.

"Let's talk about it later," she cautioned Sam, smiling innocently at the tour guide, embarrassed at having interrupted his presentation.

When they returned to the car, Georgina looked at Samantha, awaiting an explanation.

"Another one of your visions, I suppose?" she asked, cocking her head to one side.

"That man is not missing. I just know he's here in town, but for some reason, he doesn't want to be found."

"You mean he's hiding?"

"No, I don't sense that he's hiding either."

"So why is he missing? Why hasn't anyone found him or reported seeing him?"

Sam felt perplexed as she absentmindedly rubbed a finger across her cheek and down to her chin.

"That's the mystery. Maybe he doesn't know he's missing." She thought for a moment. "I bet we can find him!"

Georgiana started the car, her left arm resting lightly on the steering wheel as she turned to Sam.

"How do you know where this person is?"

Samantha tried to explain. "I don't know how I know, but it's not the first time. It's kind of like radar, like a compass in my head. I can detect a person and I'm drawn in a certain direction. That's kind of how it feels, anyway."

"I think what you are describing is called clairvoyant perception," Georgiana stated with certainty. "I looked it up for a news story on mediums once."

"I don't care what it's called; I just know we can find this man."

"I'm off tomorrow," Georgiana replied. "I can pick you up at the Bean after work. Where do you think we should start?"

"Let's head downtown and see what happens."

Georgiana nodded, turned to check the mirrors, and pulled into the street.

Saturday, Samantha had to work until noon. Georgiana picked her up at the Brown Bean. They grabbed a quick bite at a food truck and headed downtown, guided by Samantha's directional sense.

"What is your radar telling you? Are we getting close?"

Samantha looked determined as she silently pointed ahead. Soon, they came upon the city park.

"He's here," Sam said emphatically.

"There's nobody here!" Georgiana protested.

"There, on the park bench," Sam said.

Georgiana parked the car, and they cautiously approached a stranger on the park bench.

"Are you sure that's not just a homeless person?" Georgiana asked quietly.

"Hello," Sam said.

The man stayed completely still. His eyes were the only part of him that gave away his awareness of their presence. He remained silent.

Despite the long beard covering his face, Samantha recognized some of the man's facial features from the photograph at the crime museum. She turned a knowing eye at Georgiana.

"Can we do something to help you?" Sam asked.

The man raised his head to face the women.

Georgiana spoke next. "I bet you could use a good meal. Can we get you something to eat?"

"That would be nice," the man said finally.

Georgiana glanced down the street to a convenience store.

"How about a sandwich?"

The man nodded. The women looked at each other, and off they went to the convenience store to buy a sandwich.

After a few minutes, they returned with a deli sandwich and a bottle of water. As the man opened the wrapper and started on the sandwich, Sam couldn't hold back any longer.

"Are you Dr. Ming Zhang?"

The man stopped eating and looked up. "I don't think so, " he said. "Why do you ask?"

Georgiana tried to look inconspicuous as she touched her phone to take a picture.

The man was irritated. He stopped eating.

"What are you doing!" he demanded.

Georgiana tried looking innocent. "I was just checking my phone for messages," she said.

Sam looked back in Georgiana's direction. "We're sorry to bother you. We'll be going now."

With that, they walked away.

Back in the car, Georgiana looked at the picture on her phone.

"I wonder where Detective Johnson is today? I want to show him this." She pecked out a text message.

In seconds came the reply. "In my office, doing reports. Is it important?"

She switched to a voice call. "Can I stop by for a visit? It might be official business."

"Sure, why not?" came the reply.

Sam and Georgiana arrived at the police department, informed the desk sergeant that they were there to meet with the detective, and the desk sergeant directed them to his office.

"What brings you two here?" He wasn't expecting to see Samantha.

Georgiana tried to explain the reason for their visit.

"We came across a cold case you might know about. Do you remember the Dr. Zhang case? The police instructor who went missing last year?"

"I do remember that case. He was one of my instructors. We ran down what few leads we had. The security video showed him leaving the building, but he wasn't seen after that. He rode the bus from where he lived. There was no sign of anything wrong at his apartment, and none of his relatives heard from him. There were some who said he had been under stress about something, but we never got further than that."

Georgiana pulled out her phone and brought up the picture. "Does this look like him?" she asked. "We found him downtown in the park."

"Hard to tell, with the long hair and beard, but it does look a little like him. Did you talk to him?"

Sam interjected, "We asked him if he was Dr. Zhang, and all he said was I don't think so."

"That seems odd, doesn't it," the detective replied. "I suppose we could get a picture from the cold case file. Let me check. It may take me a few minutes. You stay here while I check."

With that, Detective Johnson left his office and headed down the hall to the records storeroom. He returned with a manila envelope and carefully laid the out contents on his desk. Among the various reports and papers was an eight by ten photograph, the same as the one in the mystery museum.

"Where did you say you saw him?" Johnson looked at his watch, noting the time. It would be dark soon, and likely the man would soon make his way to a homeless shelter.

"We can see if he's still in the park," Sam suggested.

Detective Johnson was curious, so they all headed downtown.

When they got to the park, they spotted the man they were looking for walking on the sidewalk. They pulled into a parking space beyond where he was.

Detective Johnson immediately noticed the man's familiar Asian appearance. They got out and waited. As the man approached, Detective Johnson spoke.

"Hello. Do I know you?" he asked.

The man looked up. "Why would you?" he asked.

At the sound of the man's voice, Johnson was now sure.

"How have you been, my old friend? Remember me? You taught me what I know about evidence."

There was a tiny spark of recognition in the man's eyes, but only that, as the man turned to leave.

"Where are you headed? Can we give you a lift?" Samantha asked.

"I'm going to the shelter," he replied, only then revealing a slight smile. It wasn't clear if he recognized detective Johnson or even if he remembered the sandwich Georgiana and Samantha had given him earlier that day.

On Monday afternoon, Detective Johnson stopped by the Brown Bean Coffee Shoppe to see Samantha. After she poured two cups of coffee, they sat down at a table. As luck would have it, Georgiana stopped by at the same time. David instinctively produced her favorite latte, and she joined Sam and the detective.

"I suppose you want to know what happened," he began. "After we dropped him off at the shelter, I did some checking. He ended up at the shelter after he was picked up wandering the streets."

"I talked him into getting a shave and a haircut. When I stopped by this morning to check on him, there was no question who he was. From what we can determine, Dr. Zhang must have had a mental breakdown. He forgot who he was. I contacted the local mental health clinic, and they said they might help him. Whether he will return to teaching is another matter, but I'm glad you showed me that picture. What I don't understand is how you two stumbled into him when you did."

Georgiana explained, "I told Sam I found out about the police museum and we decided to take the Cold Case tour."

Sam chimed in, "When we came to one exhibit, I had one of my weird flash visions. I felt certain that Dr. Zhang was in town. I talked Georgiana into looking for him. That's how we wound up at the park."

"Why did he lose his memory?" Georgiana wanted to know.

"From what I could gather from the nurse at the shelter, the doctors think he might have suffered a rare case of Dissociated Fuge State, brought on by severe stress. Nobody recognized him because nobody expected him to be wandering the streets."

"Wasn't he just an instructor?" Sam asked.

"We don't really know kinds of cases he might have been involved in."

"I'm glad you took us seriously."

"Well," Johnson said after hearing the explanation, "you two certainly make my life interesting. I'm glad I don't have to explain to the chief how I get involved in your adventures including this special case of lost and found."

Chapter Sixteen

The Missing Ingredient

When Samantha arrived for work at the Brown Bean Thursday morning, David Dillon was taping up a poster.

"Hey, David, what's going on?" Samantha asked, her voice tinged with concern.

David finished securing the poster to the window. "You haven't heard? A student went missing."

"No, I didn't. What happened?"

"Her name is Kayla Renner. She disappeared after leaving a party last weekend."

"That doesn't sound good at all. Do the police have any clues?"

"Not yet," David answered.

Sam studied the photo on the poster. A sudden chill ran down her spine as she saw flashes of a dark wooded area and the body of a young woman on the ground. The vision only lasted a few seconds. Blinking rapidly, she composed herself before David might notice.

"That's awful." Samantha said, her voice still shaky from the experience. "I hope they find her soon."

As the day went on, Sam couldn't dismiss the unsettling vision of the young woman from her mind. From the Brown Bean parking lot after work, Sam called Detective Johnson on his personal phone.

"I heard about that missing college student, Kayla Renner," she said, without preamble.

"Before you start, I can't share any details about the case beyond what we have released to the media. You can ask Georgiana about that."

"Does it count if I saw what happened to her?" Sam asked.

"What do you mean?" Johnson's voice was stern.

"I mean that I had a vision of what happened to her," she answered.

"You need to be careful about this one. A life is in danger."

"That's what I wanted to tell you. I don't think she is alive."

Johnson was silent for a moment. "Perhaps we need to discuss this in my office."

"I'm off work, so I can stop by now."

Detective Ronald Johnson was waiting in his office when Samantha got there.

"What's this about a vision? What do you think you saw?"

"When I saw the picture in the missing person poster David put up at the coffee shop, I had a sudden image of a body in the woods."

"I know your *special talent* has been helpful, but you've never claimed to see a murder victim. Are you sure you want to go that far?"

"I can't help it. I have a strong feeling about this one."

"I can't discuss the case with you, but we have to assume she's alive until we have reason to believe otherwise." Johnson gestured to a map on the wall of his office. "As far as we know, she's out there somewhere."

Samantha studied the map. Her attention focused on a location near the college campus.

"I've never tried to do this before, but I think you might want to start here." Sam pointed to a place on the map.

"We're still looking for a missing person, not a murder victim. I'm sorry."

Sam was clearly disappointed, but she understood the reality of his situation with a new police chief.

Still convinced the missing student was somewhere in the woods behind the college campus, Samantha felt compelled to do her own investigation. It would be dark soon, and Georgiana would be tied up on assignments until after dark. She was on her own.

Determined to get an answer, Sam drove to the college campus. The air under the trees was dense and strangely silent. Only the occasional crunch of leaves beneath her feet broke the stillness. Her heart beat faster with each step, though she couldn't shake the strange force pulling her. Sam walked carefully through the thick woods, tensing from the cold of the fall evening air.

Sam soon found herself in a small clearing. A dark shape in the open area drew her attention. She took a few steps and stopped. There, among the branches and fallen leaves, was a body. Samantha's throat tightened; her eyes locked on the scene in front of her.

After a few moments, she used her phone to take a photo. In the map application, she took a screenshot. Still in shock, Sam sent the pictures to Detective Johnson's number. Her phone immediately rang with a call from the detective.

Before Johnson could say hello, Sam blurted out, "I found a body in the woods."

"Where are you now?" he demanded.

"I'm in the college parking lot," Sam answered.

"Stay where you are. I'll have officers are on the way."

When two officers arrived, Sam answered their questions before guiding them through the woods to the location of the body. They took her to the police station, but she could leave after Detective Johnson intervened. An officer took her back to the parking lot where she left her car.

Visions of the scene in the woods haunted Samantha as she tried to sleep that night. She kept wondering what could have led to such a tragic death.

The next day at work, Sam avoided looking at the poster. The police hadn't yet announced that they had found a body. Perhaps it was not the missing college student? Perhaps they needed to notify the family first.

At the end of her shift, when Sam retrieved her purse, she found a text message from Detective Jonson asking that she come to the police station.

Upon arrival, the officers directed Sam to a small room. Detective Johnson soon joined her and introduced Captain James Lawson. As the conversation began, it was clear the police chief suspected Samantha of having some involvement in the crime.

"You expect us to believe you just *found* the body?" Lawson demanded.

Sam protested. "Like I told Detective Johnson, when I saw the picture on the poster, I had a vision of a body in the woods. I told him about it but he said that was not enough to start a search. When I went there, I felt a force pulling me to where I found the body."

The chief stared at Sam in disbelief. "So, you saw it in your head, did you? Let me get this straight—you 'sensed' the exact location? I've got detectives looking for a missing person, but somehow you managed to stumble on a dead body? That's not adding up."

Captain Lawson spent the next hour questioning Samantha about what connection she might have with the college or the missing student. Sam understood why others might view her explanation skeptically.

During the interrogation, Detective Johnson was uncharacteristically silent, perhaps intimidated by his new boss.

Eventually, Sam was allowed to leave.

That night, Samantha watched the news. The report only mentioned that the police had received a "tip from a concerned individual."

The report said a preliminary examination by the medical examiner showed the cause of death appeared consistent with strangulation. Investigators also found evidence that someone had dragged the body a considerable distance, but they could not determine the murder location.

Samantha was glad to see Georgiana the next morning at the Brown Bean.

"We need to talk about something," she said to Georgiana as she delivered her latte.

She asked David to take over the sales counter so they could go to a back table to talk.

Sam began, "You heard about the missing college student they found yesterday, right?"

"Yeah, that was sad. The police aren't telling us much."

"You know how I sometimes have these visions of things,"

"Go on. Where is this going?" Georgiana asked.

"I had a picture in my mind of a body in the woods."

"Did you tell the police?"

"That's the thing, the police chief thinks I had something to do with it."

Georgiana questioned, looking puzzled. "What could possibly be his reason for thinking that?"

"Because I found the body and told the police where it was."

"Oh." Georgiana was thoughtful. "So *that* was the tip. Well, I had a tip of my own. One of Kayla's friends who went to high school with her called me at the station. She said before Kayla went missing, her old boyfriend had been bothering her."

"Wow, do we know who he is?" Sam asked.

"She said his name is Jason Morrow. The one who called me shared a prom picture he posted on a group chat last year."

"A picture doesn't mean anything."

"It might if it has *forever mine* written on it. I think he is seriously obsessed."

"Do the police know about any of this?" Sam asked. "That might be a clue to solving her murder."

"I think the college students are afraid to contact the police."

Sam was adamant. "We need to tell Detective Johnson what we know. After all, there's a killer out there somewhere."

"That's exactly what I have in mind," Georgiana replied.

Detective Johnson looked up from his desk when Georgiana placed a printout of the prom photo on his desk.

"What's this?" he asked.

"I think that could be the killer," she said, pointing to the picture. "One of Kayla's friends sent that to me. That's Jason Morrow. Notice what it says: forever mine. Kayla's friend told me he had been bothering her. I'm guessing he confronted her at her apartment."

"I see what you mean. That name never came up in our investigation."

"So, you're going to arrest Jason Morrow?"

"It's not that simple. None of what I'm telling you now is for public disclosure, you understand, and I'll trust you to respect that. When we checked Kayla's apartment, it was unlocked and her purse and phone were still there. That would suggest she knew her attacker. We asked about a boyfriend, but nothing came up. This picture might be enough to get a judge to let us unlock Kayla's phone to check for any threats. It would also take a court order to get data from the group chat. But I think we could be on the way to solving the case." He winked. "Captain Lawson may be in for some surprises."

It was more than two weeks later when Georgiana got a news release announcing a break in the investigation and the arrest of Jason Morrow.

Strangulation often indicates a crime of passion. Text messages found on the victim's phone pointed to the boyfriend. Confronted with the evidence, Morrow had confessed.

Jason admitted going to Kayla's apartment, hoping to resume their relationship. He convinced her to go for a walk to talk things over. At some point, Kayla broke the news that she was no longer interested in him. Mason became enraged and attacked Kayla in a dark section of the parking lot. He admitted, dragging her body into the woods.

At the Brown Bean, Georgiana handed Samantha the news release.

"They arrested the boyfriend," she said. "We did it!"

"That prom picture was the missing ingredient," Sam added.

"That, and your vision of the where the body was found."

Samantha smiled. "I wonder if we will ever convince Captain Lawson?"

"I doubt it," Detective Johnson said as he slipped in unnoticed behind Georgiana. "He says she needs to stay out of police business. I told him Sam's special gift has come in handy a few times, but he's having none of it."

Georgiana smiled at Samantha. "He'll figure it out someday."

Chapter Seventeen

Mocha Mirage

Samantha had seen the man placing the order several times before. He was hard to miss in his expensive three-piece suit with an attitude to match. The man's meticulously groomed appearance radiated confidence. His dark brown hair was combed back neatly, showing a hint of gray at the temples.

Sam handed him his order and completed the sale. He paid in cash.

"I don't believe I haven't properly introduced myself," the man said. "I'm Gregory Winslow," as he handed Sam a fancy business card with raised gold lettering and a company logo.

"Nice to meet you, Mr. Winslow. I've seen you here quite a few times. Do you work nearby?" Sam asked.

"I'm a financial consultant and I have several clients in the area. I help people take advantage of investment opportunities."

Samantha sensed a strong negative energy. She had the distinct impression the man was all polish and no silver.

"That's nice," Sam replied, hoping to end the conversation. She dropped the business card in an apron pocket. Sam smiled as she turned her attention to the next customer in line. "Who's next? May I help you?"

Winslow got the hint and walked away with his Chocolate Mocha.

Arthur Hopkins, an older gentleman, was a regular customer at The Brown Bean.

Winslow's attention quickly refocused on Mr. Hopkins.

"Hello, I'm Greg Winslow. I hope you don't mind if I join you."

Hopkins looked on with some curiosity as Winslow took a seat at his table.

"Glad to meet you, Mr. Winslow. I'm Arthur."

Winslow launched right into his pitch. "These days, you can't even be sure about the banks. In the right place, even a very small investment can bring surprising returns. I have just the opportunity for you. With the right investment, you can double your savings. I can provide you with an opportunity to secure your future."

"How can you do that?" Hopkins asked, curiously.

"It's simple, really," he answered. Winslow reached into the briefcase he was carrying and produced a glossy brochure, which he handed to Mr. Hopkins.

As Hopkins glanced at the brochure, Winslow continued talking, pointing to the brochure.

"Our investors have been pulling in profits month after month. What would you think of a guaranteed 15% return?"

"How can it be guaranteed? What's the catch?"

"No catch! It's all about leveraging. I've been doing this for years. Most people don't know how to manage risk. That's why they lose money. My system minimizes exposure across multiple industries. You're lucky, because I can get you in on the ground floor."

Georgiana strained to overhear the conversation from her place at the sales counter. She went to clear some nearby tables so she could hear the conversation better.

"I must admit, it does sound interesting. What kind of investment are we talking about?" Arthur asked.

"That's your choice, of course," Winslow replied. "Most of my clients begin with $10,000, but you could start with as little as $5,000, but I warn you, this opportunity may not be available for long."

"I'll need to think about it,"

"By all means. Here's my card. I have another appointment, but you can call me any time," Winslow promised, glancing at his slim gold watch as he got up to leave.

Mr. Hopkins finished his coffee and went on his way, leaving the fancy brochure behind.

Sam was concerned that Arthur Hopkins could become the victim of a shady scheme. She reached for the brochure on the table, but as she touched it, she felt a sudden chill and sensed a mocha-brown aura of greed. She quickly stuffed it into her apron pocket.

That afternoon after work, Sam sat at a table with the fancy brochure. The first thing she noticed was there was no company address, only a website for the investment company, along with vague promises of "guaranteed returns" and bonus incentives for introducing others to the program. In the small print, of course, was a disclaimer that profits depended on "market conditions."

Sam felt a strong empathy for people who could become victims of the scheme. She knew something needed to be done, and she hoped Detective Johnson could be the one to do it. Sam dug into her apron pocket for the business card with Winslow's phone number. She had a plan for the next time she saw Detective Johnson.

That opportunity came sooner than expected when, in the next few moments, the detective walked into the Brown Bean. After Sandra brought his order, Sam waved him over to where she was sitting.

"I have something you might interest you," she said, waving the brochure. She handed the brochure to Johnson.

"What's this?" he asked as he looked it over.

"It feels like something illegal," Sam answered.

Johnson glanced at the brochure and nodded. "You're right. It has the look of a standard Ponzi scheme. Where did you get this?" he asked.

Sam handed him the business card. "Gregory Winslow. He's been talking to some of our customers lately."

Johnson studied the brochure a bit more. "There's a possibility of securities fraud. I'd like to see what he's up to, but we would need evidence for the U.S. Attorney. Let me see what I can do."

Later that week, Gregory Winslow showed up at the Brown Bean, accompanied by a well-dressed man in his mid-forties. Winslow ordered his Chocolate Mocha and a black coffee for his guest, and the two selected a table for their discussion. Sam decided some nearby tables needed to be cleaned and listened in on the conversation.

"This is your once in a lifetime opportunity," Winslow was saying.

"Is this investment registered with the proper authorities?" his guest asked.

"That's the beauty of it! These are offshore opportunities. There's no government interference!"

"Can you explain how the profits are generated?" the man asked.

Winslow pulled out the same brochure. "Better than that, our strategy ensures consistent returns. You can see the testimonials from satisfied investors. You many recognize some names."

"What if I need money for expenses?"

Winslow smiled. "You can withdraw your funds at any time without penalties."

The guest kept asking more and more questions. Samantha suspected a trap was being set. She smiled to herself and went back to the sales counter as the conversation between Winslow and his new prospect continued.

By the end of the week, Samantha realized she had not seen Mr. Winslow. She suspected she might know the reason. The answer was not long in coming.

"Score another one for the good guys," Georgiana said as she raised her latte in a mock toast to Samantha. "Detective Johnson told me about your friend, Mr. Winslow. It seems the Federal agents got a search warrant and raided his office. They came back with financial statements, names, business records, and a lot more. It turns out he was laundering money through a network of shell companies in a classic Ponzi scheme. He used some of the money from new investors to pay dividends to the earlier investors."

"Where is he now?" Sam asked.

"He's in a federal holding facility awaiting trial in Atlanta."

"That happened pretty fast. Don't these things usually take years?"

"That's where it gets interesting. Winslow is not who he says he is. His real name is Gregory Weston. The Feds were about to close in on him in Atlanta when he disappeared. That's when he turned up here as Gregory Winslow, still playing the same game. When they figured out who he was, they had an undercover agent set up a meeting. The agent turned in his evidence to the U.S. Attorney. After that, they moved quickly."

"At least he won't be cheating any more people," Sam said.

"I don't know if Captain Lawson will ever give you credit, but he should," Georgiana added. "But I'm sure Detective Johnson is grateful for your tip."

Sam was thoughtful. "I knew I was right about him. All the fancy talk about big profits! It was all a mirage: a chocolate mocha mirage."

Chapter Eighteen

The Espresso Paradox

When Samantha awoke that morning, she had a strange feeling. For one thing, her apartment was different. She saw decorations she did not recognize.

Glancing at the clock, she got up and began her normal routine. She had to get ready for work. After her shower, she got dressed and grabbed the yogurt container from the refrigerator and scooped out a bowl full and popped a slice of bread in the toaster.

Sunlight was just peeking through the kitchen window shades as the toast popped up from the toaster. Finishing the last of the yogurt, Sam rinsed out the bowl and left it in the sink to dry. She stuck the toast in her mouth as she grabbed a light coat, locked up the apartment, and headed out to the parking lot and her car.

Still, the strange feeling persisted.

Driving to the Brown Bean, Sam noticed more things seemed strangely unfamiliar.

Samantha arrived at the coffee shop, parked at the rear of the coffee shop lot as usual, and entered the Brown Bean Coffee Shoppe through the back door.

David was at the register, taking orders from early customers.

"Where's Marge?" Sam asked.

David looked perplexed.

"What do you mean? Marge has been out ever since her mother became ill. Are you OK?"

"Sorry, sometimes I forget." (Sam was pretending). "It just doesn't feel the same without Marge, does it."

Sam was trying to adjust her mind when Georgiana rushed in.

"A Grande almond milk latte with a shot of vanilla syrup, to go," she told David at the sales count

Sam adjusted her apron as she emerged from the back room.

"What brings you by so early?" Sam asked. "Chasing a hot story?"

Georgiana gave her a strange look. "You know I can't stand the coffee they have at the studio."

Sam was thoroughly confused. "You're working in the studio!? Wow! When did that happen?"

Georgiana stopped and stared at Sam for a moment, one hand on her hip. "Only about a year ago. Are you alright? Sometimes I wonder about you, Sam."

Georgiana's odd expression remained as David brought her order. Georgiana paid and left in just as much of a hurry as when she came in.

Samantha's mind was spinning, trying to adjust. She felt lost and bewildered. Her world was completely turned around.

"You gonna work today?" David barked.

"Sorry. You want me on the register?"

"That would be nice." David's response seemed terse and condescending. David was always calm and polite to Sam. She wondered what would cause such a drastic change. Sam decided it must be from the pressure of filling in as manager while Marge was away.

On her way to take over at the register, Sam glanced at the menu board and noticed several unfamiliar items. The list included Pumpkin Spice and Gingerbread Lattes along with Peppermint Mocha.

A customer stepped up to the register. "I'll have a Café au Lait"

Samantha scanned an unfamiliar order screen until she found the selection. At least the recipe was simple enough.

As she worked, Sam kept trying to make sense of the situation. How could it happen? Had she somehow stepped through a portal? Was she caught in a terrible dream?

Sam poured two shots of espresso into a cup and mixed in half-and-half from a carton in the cooler. The customer took a sip and placed the cup on the counter with an unhappy stare. Sam's distraction caused her to make a mistake on the order. She forgot to add the chocolate syrup,. Sam realized her error and added the missing ingredient.

Out of the corner of her eye, Sam saw David had seen what happened.

"Sorry!" she said to both David and the customer. David shrugged and shook his head, and walked back to the manager's office.

As Sam glanced up from the register, she saw a short man standing at the counter. He was dressed in a well-worn tweed jacket with elbow patches over a brightly colored vest. He tied a patterned scarf loosely around his neck. The outfit seemed out of place in the warm spring weather.

"How about a Mocha Breve?" the man asked, looking up at the menu board.

Once again, Sam scanned the menu screen and pressed the button for the selection.

"Will there be anything else I can get for you today?" she asked.

The man simply smiled.

"Why are you looking at me that way?" Sam asked, trying not to seem rude.

"Because I know your secret," he said.

Sam turned her head with a puzzled look on her face, but without speaking, she turned to the back counter. Sam poured a small amount of milk into a shallow saucepan and placed it on the hot plate burner. After a few moments, small bubbles appeared in the milk. As soon as it did, she poured equal amounts of milk and strong coffee into a cup and gently stirred it before taking it to the sales counter.

"And what secret would that be?" Sam asked.

"Time is a river, and sometimes it flows in a different direction. You just have to know how to swim against the current. This place is like a beacon for those who slip between worlds."

"I don't understand," Sam responded.

The strange man looked back to be sure no one was in line behind him as he whispered, "This is not really your world, is it."

Sam tilted her head as she looked into his eyes intently, searching for answers.

"You don't even know me," she protested.

Leaning closer, he continued, "Let's just say, I'm a fellow traveler. I must warn you, the longer you remain, the more fragile your own reality becomes."

Sam whispered, "Let's assume for a moment that I know what you are talking about, and I'm still not sure that I do. How to I solve ... my problem?"

"You must find a key, a common connection "

The strange man turned to look about the room.

"What are we looking for, " Sam asked, curiously.

"You must connect with an object that transcends dimensions."

"I think you mean old," she answered. She pointed to a display on the back wall. "Like that antique coffee pot."

The strange man nodded.

Samantha walked over, reached for the old pot, and took it down. She turned to find the strange man was behind her. The man nodded approval of her selection.

"What do I need to do?" she asked.

The man stood close and whispered instructions. "Hold the object with both hands. Be conscious of its weight."

Sam did as she was told and waited for more instructions as the man continued.

"Close your eyes and clear your mind."

"OK," Sam responded.

"Now visualize something from your reality, some person, or thing that is a part of your world."

Grasping the old pot in both hands, she closed her eyes and concentrated her thoughts as she envisioned returning to her own dimension.

Samantha felt a wave of energy surging through her body. Sweat formed on her face and neck.

She heard a voice.

"Are you alright? What are you doing to that old pot?"

It was Marge!

Samantha cautiously opened her eyes. Could it be?

It was Marge! It really was Marge!

Sam looked around. The strange little man was also nowhere to be seen and the unfamiliar items were no longer on the menu board.

Sam felt a wave of relief sweeping over her.

"Are you alright?" Marge repeated.

"Yes," Sam replied as she took a deep breath, savoring the familiar scent of coffee and pastries.

Still holding the old pot, she reached up and put it back in its place on the shelf, giving it a gentle tap with her fingers.

That was when she noticed a small piece of folded paper tucked into the back of the shelf. Out of curiosity, she opened it and read the message inside:

"Reality is a tapestry woven from our perceptions."

Sam thought for a moment about what it might mean, then tucked the note in her pocket and went back to work.

Chapter Nineteen

Mind Over Mocha

Samantha became aware of a dark, perhaps even a deep green or black aura surrounding the customer, who stepped up to the sales counter at the Brown Bean Coffee Shoppe.

"Excuse me?" the woman said, as Sam realized she might have been staring.

"Yes," Sam responded. "What can we make for you?"

"I'll have a Black Velvet Mocha," the woman said as she stood studying the large menu board hanging from the ceiling behind Samantha's head.

"We'll be happy to make that for you, but it will take about 15 minutes. Would that be alright?"

The woman nodded in agreement and held her credit card ready to complete the sale. Sam punched the keys, and the woman waved the card over the sensor. As the machine generated the receipt, Sam asked, "What name should we put on the order?"

The woman was tall, possibly in her early thirties, with dark brown hair pulled back into a simple ponytail. Her outfit consisted of a knee-length navy blue dress with sleeves.

"Hannah," the woman said, glancing briefly at her electronic watch as she moved to the stand-up counter next to the door.

Samantha handed the order slip to David and continued processing orders for customers in the line.

Sam again turned to concentrate on the woman waiting for the mocha at the stand-up counter. The woman looked nervous. She sensed a dark gray aura surrounding the woman. As Sam wondered what it might mean, she heard a voice in her head.

"Remain calm. Don't arouse suspicion," the voice said. Samantha wondered what it meant.

"Hannah," Sam said as she motioned to the woman that her order was ready. At first, the woman did not respond until Sam repeated her name. This time, she picked up the order and left the coffee shop.

Samantha wondered what the strange voice in her head might mean.

Sam thought no more about it until the woman returned the next day.

Once again, Sam was able to intercept her thoughts.

"What can I do if the police start asking questions?"

This time, the woman ordered a plain black coffee and a pastry to go. As she swiped the credit card over the sensor, Samantha held down a key on the order screen, causing the payment to fail. The woman tried scanning the card once again, but the payment was blocked. The woman looked nervous and confused.

"Let me try," Sam offered, holding out her hand. The woman gave Sam the card. Samantha lifted her finger off the pause button as she pretended to examine the card, careful to hold it where the security camera would record it. Sam wiped the edge of the card with a napkin and handed it back to the customer.

"Here. Try it again."

This time the payment went through. Sam filled a cup with coffee from the pot next to the counter and handed it to the woman. As the woman turned to leave, Sam jotted down the name "Hannah Everett" on a napkin before stuffing it in her apron pocket.

Sam was still thinking about the voice in her head when Detective Johnson stopped by. Sam poured his coffee and handed it to him.

"Got a minute?" Sam asked.

Johnson knew she had something on her mind.

"Sure," he said.

There were no more customers waiting, so Sam joined him at the stand-up counter and thought about how she would address the issue.

"There's a customer who's been acting strange."

Johnson was initially skeptical. "In what way?" he asked.

"She was acting nervous. Then, when I called her name to let her know her order was ready, it was like she forgot who she was."

"You didn't get her full name, did you?" Johnson asked.

Sam smiled and pulled the napkin from the pocket in her apron.

Johnson looked at the name on the napkin. "Hannah Everett. OK, I'll check it out."

Samantha was at home in the afternoon when she got a call from Detective Johnson.

"I ran that name through our records, and I found something interesting. The Hannah Everett in our files is dead. She was the victim of a homicide last month in Atlanta. Too bad we don't have a picture of the woman you saw using that credit card."

"Actually, we do," Sam replied. "I pretended the card didn't go through and got her to hand it to me. I held it up, so our security camera could see it, before I gave it back to her. The security guys can find the video for you. You already know how to reach them, right?"

"It's in my file. I'll let you know what I find."

The next morning, Georgiana stopped by for her regular order.

"Anything different going on with you?" she asked.

Sam scanned the customers to be sure 'Hannah' was not among them

"We have a dead person as a customer."

Georgiana laughed. "OK, you'll need to explain that one to me."

"A woman was acting very nervous. I had a bad feeling, so I managed to read the name from her credit card. I told Detective Johnson about it. He looked it up and told me the person with that name was dead."

"So, the credit card was stolen from a dead person?"

"That's what it sounds like to me. The detective is checking the video from the security company."

"I would be interested to know what he finds out." Georgiana raised the cup with her almond latte as she opened the door to go back to work.

Just then, David waved to Sam. He held up the receiver of the store's phone and said, "Call for you."

Sam picked up the phone. It was Detective Johnson.

"I checked the video. Hannah Everett was a sixty-year-old blonde. The woman in your video looks a lot like someone who knew the victim. Does your mystery woman come every day?" he asked.

"She's usually here a little after nine most days. Why?"

"I might be stopping by to about that time tomorrow. Don't say my name. Pretend you don't know me."

Just after nine, Detective Johnson ordered a coffee and took up a table in the front corner of the coffee shop, where he could see the order counter and the sidewalk outside the front window. And he waited.

At last, the mystery woman entered and went to place an order.

Johnson looked out the window, where a plain-clothes officer was sitting in an unmarked car. The officer got out of the car and moved toward the door of the Brown Bean. When the officer was in position at the door, Detective Johnson walked up behind the woman at the order counter.

She was about to pay for her order with the credit card when Johnson reached around and took it from her hand.

"Excuse me," he said. "We would like to ask you a few questions."

Startled, the woman turned around. Glancing toward the exit, she could see the officer blocking the way.

Suddenly gaining her composure, the woman smiled.

"Of course. Is there a problem?"

"The problem is, you are under arrest and charged with using a stolen credit card."

Immediately, the woman's mood shifted as the officer approached and escorted her to the unmarked vehicle.

They brought the suspect into the interrogation room at the downtown police department. The room was two shades of gray, with the darker shade starting midway down the wall, illuminated by parallel fluorescent light fixtures. There was a video camera mounted on one wall. Inside the room, there were three wooden chairs and a metal table. On the left side of the room was a large one-way window. A microphone pointed down from the center of the ceiling.

Detective Johnson entered the room carrying a file folder and sat in the chair opposite the suspect. An officer stood next to the door. The suspect sat at the table with her arms crossed over her chest.

"Good afternoon. The officer who brought you in explained your Miranda rights. Do you still want to talk to us?"

"Sure. I didn't do anything. I was just trying to pay for my coffee," she replied.

Detective Johnson leafed through the papers in the file before pulling out a photograph. He placed the photo on the table in front of the suspect. "Miss Briggs, this is a security photo of you. According to our fingerprint records, your name is Lena Biggs, but that wasn't the name on the credit card you were using, was it."

The suspect glanced at the picture and answered, "So?"

"So, can you explain why you were using Hannah Everett's credit card?"

"Maybe she gave it to me."

"How did you come to know Hannah Everett?" Johnson asked.

"I didn't have anywhere to go so she let me stay in her house," Briggs replied.

"I think you stole that credit card from her. We could ask her, but I'm afraid she turned up dead a few weeks ago. You wouldn't know anything about that, would you?"

Briggs was silent, squirming in her chair.

"Atlanta police think they have enough evidence to tie you to the crime."

"I didn't poison her. It must have been someone else," Riggs protested.

Johnson turned to the officer standing next to the door.

"Did I say anything about poisoning," he asked the officer. The officer shook his head.

"Miss Riggs, I believe we're about done for today. We have already established that you committed credit card theft, but I'm afraid we're going to have to hold you on suspicion of murder until the evidence arrives from Atlanta police. The officer here will be accompanying you to your accommodation."

The next morning, Georgiana had some news for Samantha.

"I just left the news conference," she told Samantha. "The woman turned out to be Lena Briggs. Besides using a stolen credit card, the police in Atlanta put the pieces together and charged her with murdering the woman whose name was on the credit card she was using. They say Briggs put poison in a strawberry shortcake when Everett refused to give her money. I still don't understand how you caught on to her so quickly."

Samantha winked and smiled. "Sometimes it's not just the caffeine that keeps us sharp, it's a bit of mind over mocha."

Chapter Twenty

A Taste of Justice

Samantha looked up from the coffee shop sales counter as Georgiana burst through the door.

"You look like a woman on a mission. I'll start on your usual and you can tell me all about it," Sam said as she turned to the back counter to prepare the order.

Georgiana smiled and tucked a stray strand of her auburn hair behind her ear, drumming her fingers on the counter as she waited for Sam to make her Grande almond milk latte. With a shot of vanilla syrup, of course.

Sam set the cup on the counter and rang up the sale. Georgiana waved her card across the sensor and picked up the cup.

"If you don't mind me saying it, you look like you didn't get a lot of sleep. Is it about a big story?"

"You could say that," Georgiana replied somewhat dismissively. She leaned in to Sam and whispered, "I got a tip about a superior court judge. They think he is fixing cases."

Sam's eyes opened wide as she whispered, "He's taking bribes?"

"That's what it looks like. My tip pointed out several cases where the defendants got off way too easy. Last night I dug into the county court clerk website, but I didn't find anything solid to go on."

Sam was concerned. "Powerful people could be involved. You need to talk to Detective Johnson about it? Besides, ruffling the wrong feathers could be be dangerous."

"What could I tell him? I've got nothing but suspicions and rumors."

"You don't know where the tip came from or who it is? Are you sure you can believe them?"

"The station has a secure tip form on the website. It runs through a VPN or Virtual Private Network. It works like Signal or Telegram. That's why they contacted the station. I think they were afraid to contact the police directly."

"Who is the judge?" Sam asked.

Georgiana opened the photo app on her phone and flipped through a few images before turning the phone over to show a picture to Sam.

Georgiana looked behind her before she spoke. "It's Judge Eugene Whitaker. I looked him up. I got this off the county court website."

Samantha held the phone and carefully studied the picture.

"Hold on, I'm getting something," Sam said, holding up her hand and closing her eyes. A vision flashed in her mind, lasting only a few moments. "There's a ledger, a kind of spiral bound notebook with a black cover. I see dates and names. Somebody's keeping track of the bribes."

"You can get that from looking at a picture of the judge?"

"I can't explain it, but I know a record book is the key that ties it all together."

Georgiana glanced at her watch. "I gotta get to an assignment downtown. I'll call Detective Johnson later and let him know what we have."

Later, Georgiana sent a text to Detective Johnson about the tip. Johnson texted back, asking her to stop by his office the next day before she went to the TV station.

Detective Johnson's office was small but surprisingly uncluttered, nothing like the typical detective's dingy office portrayed on some television shows.

"We've had our own suspicions for some time," he admitted as she sat in a chair before his desk, "but, all we had was rumors. Nothing concrete to go on,"

"Samantha seems to think they're keeping a record in some kind of ledger," Georgiana told him. "I did some checking on the cases mentioned in the tip. They all had one thing in common: charges against the defendant were dropped on technicalities."

"Let me see what I can do."

"I trust you'll let me know when the time comes," Georgiana replied as she got up to leave.

Johnson nodded as he went back to the paperwork on his desk.

Detective Johnson met with his boss, police chief Captain James Lawson, to outline a plan for a sting operation targeting the judge and others involved in the bribery operation.

"How do you propose to build a case?" the chief asked.

"We've got an undercover resource who can pose as a desperate parent in a high-stakes custody case. There is reason to suspect a certain bail bondsmen is the point of contact. We'll set the bait and see what happens. We have someone in the courthouse who can create a case number."

"All I can say is, you better be right," the chief responded. "We don't need to make any unnecessary enemies in the courthouse."

The undercover agent visited the bail bondsman, Clint Donovan.

Donovan, in his 50s, was charismatic and well-connected. He had an expensive taste in suits and often handled high-profile cases.

The plan was coming together.

And then it didn't.

The undercover agent called Detective Johnson.

"Our target called off the deal. I think he was tipped off. I suspect there was a leak."

Detective Johnson gritted his teeth. "I was afraid this might happen," he said. "Maybe we can still save it. Let me see what I can do."

After lunch, as Detective Johnson was heading back to his office, there was a text message from Georgiana. She had more information about the case. He closed the door to make the call.

"There may be something more to the case than we thought," Georgiana told him.

Johnson's eyebrows rose. "How so?".

"Sam had another vision about the ledger. The judge doesn't have it."

"Do we know who does?"

"The strange part is, Sam's intuition is that it's someone close to you."

"That's interesting. That would certainly explain the leak. Thank you and thank Sam for me. Let me know if she comes up with anything else."

"Sure thing, detective."

"Oh, and I did some checking on the judge. Did you know he wasn't elected? Judge Whitaker got a mid-term appointment by the governor. Guess who was the head of the judicial nominating committee? The bail bondsman's brother, Harold Donovan. It also turns out Clint Donovan was a big supporter of the governor's campaign."

"That fills in a lot of the missing dots, but there's still one important dot missing."

"The person Sam said was close to you?" Georgiana asked.

"Exactly. I would like to know if Samantha can tell us anything more about that mysterious ledger."

As Johnson ended the call with Georgiana, he leaned back in his chair, going over the facts of the case and trying to connect the dots.

Johnson looked at the time on his phone. By now, Samantha would be heading home after work. He called her number.

"Hi, Sam, are you where you can talk?" he asked.

"I'm just pulling up to my apartment. Why?"

"Would you mind if I stop by? I want to explore any other details you might have about the case we're working on. I would rather not discuss it on the phone or at my office."

"Sure. See you then," she said, walking to her apartment.

It wasn't long before the detective arrived at Sam's address. He knocked on the door and Sam invited him in.

"I don't know what more I can tell you about that ledger. Like I told Georgiana, I only see flashes in my mind."

"If you don't mind, can you add any details about this ledger you are seeing?"

Johnson watched as Sam's eyes closed, and she concentrated.

"The ledger is in some kind of box. A file box, perhaps. It's in a box on a shelf." Sam sighed, "I'm sorry, that's all I'm getting. I know it's probably not much help."

The detective thought for a moment, then he gave Samantha a knowing wink. "Thank you. That may be the detail we needed."

Back at his office, Detective Johnson logged into the department's evidence management system. He paused for a moment at the search box before typing in "Clint Donovan." A case file matched this name, with a description listed as "suspicion of bribery." Investigators identified the evidence as a financial document. As he pieced together the information, connections began forming.

As Johnson had suspected, the box Samantha saw in her vision was a file box in the department's own evidence locker.

Before closing the file, he scrolled to the end. There was the last dot: the officer assigned to the case was Detective Marcus Reeves. That explains how Donovan received a tip about the raid.

The next step was to check into the box of evidence. The evidence storage locker resembled a bank vault. Detective Johnson signed into the secure system on a keypad that included a fingerprint scanner. There was a strong metallic click as the LED blinked green. Johnson turned the handle and pulled open the heavy metal door.

He searched the rows of boxes arranged on metal storage shelves until he found one matching the file number. He pulled down the box and placed it on a table in the center of the room. Brushing off the dust, he opened it. There it was: the mysterious black ledger. It listed dates, names, and amounts. In the last column were the names of various public officials, including a county sheriff and a judge: Judge Eugene Whitaker.

The evidence was in the last place anyone would look.

Detective Johnson took several pictures of the ledger before putting it back in the box on the shelf.

For Johnson, the job did not end there; it was just beginning. He wrote out a detailed case summary and included photos of the ledger.

His first stop was the District Attorney's office, and a trusted prosecutor Johnson had known from college. That step would be required to establish probable cause for arrest for each of the suspects.

Because the case involved a superior court judge, Johnson needed to petition a judge in another jurisdiction. After that, the next step would be to arrange for the arrests to be made simultaneously to avoid anyone being tipped off.

Arresting Donovan would be straightforward. The others would be more difficult to arrange.

The arrest of Reeves, the detective, would need to be handled by officers with no professional or personal connections to the suspect.

Arresting the judge required coordination with state or federal marshals.

The arrest of the bail bondsman, Donovan, would need to take place after the other two suspects were in custody.

Once the arrests were completed, the District Attorney held a press conference to announce the charges.

Georgiana had a knowing smile when she received the email notification of the press conference as she mumbled to herself: "The judge will get his own taste of justice"

Samantha's connection to the case remained a secret, shared only by Georgiana and Detective Johnson.

TIM TROTT
The Psychic
Barista
Book 2

Chapter Twenty-One

Preview

Here is a sneak preview from the next book in the Psychic Barista series:

The Mentor

It was late morning, and the stream of customers had dwindled to one or two at a time.

An older woman stood in front of Samantha at the sales counter. Her blonde hair gently framing her face. She wore a delicate, light colored dress, hinting at an older style, or perhaps a quiet nod to a bygone era. Her features were gentle but graceful. She seemed calm and observant.

"I would like a green tea, please," she said.

Sam rang up the sale, and the woman slid her card through the reader. "Is that for here?"

The woman nodded. "It will be a few minutes before your tea is ready. Find a seat, and I'll bring it to your table."

Turning to the electric kettle, Sam selected a temperature of 175 degrees. The automatic shutoff prevented the water from boiling. Next, she placed the green tea leaves in a strainer and poured the water through the strainer into a small teapot, and set an electronic timer to let it steep for three minutes. When the tea was ready, she placed the cup on a small tray with packets of sugar and a small jug of honey, and delivered it to where the woman was sitting, placing the tea tray on the table.

Sam felt a tingle as the woman gently touched her hand. She looked up, meeting the woman's gaze.

"You have the gift," the woman said.

"Excuse me?"

"I can sense you have discovered your paranormal senses." The woman smiled. "I am Celeste, and I can help you."

Sam wondered how this strange woman could know so much about her from a simple touch. Sam became aware of the muffled voices of customers, masked by the smooth jazz music playing from the radio on the front counter. She hoped none of the customers would overhear their conversation.

Sam stood motionless, hesitating before moving to sit opposite the strange woman.

"I'm Samantha. What do you mean? How can you help me?"

"I'm a practicing psychic, and I sense what you are going through. There is no need to fear. You have been given your abilities for a purpose. I would like to be your mentor."

"I'll admit, some of it does freak me out," Sam said in a whisper.

"Hey!" David's voice rose above the music and the surrounding voices. "Hey," he repeated, "Sam, you're needed at the front counter."

Sam smiled. "I have to go," she said, still maintaining cautious eye contact, even as she slowly got up from the chair.

(To be continued in Book 2)

For Readers and Book Club Discussions:

1. Which story was your favorite, and why?

2. How does Samantha's psychic ability influence her interactions with others? Do you think it's a gift or a burden?

3. The stories balance cozy mystery with paranormal elements. How well do these genres blend in this collection?

4. How does the setting of *The Brown Bean Coffee Shoppe* enhance the tone of the stories?

5. Did any of the mysteries surprise you with a twist? If so, which ones and why?

Please review!

Please take a few moments to write a nice review where you purchased it and recommend it to your friends and social media followers!

You can also find a review form on my website at:
TimTrottWrites.com

About the Author

Tim Trott grew up in the tiny community of Clarcona, Florida, a single four-way stop intersection between Winter Garden and Apopka, just outside of Orlando. Tim began writing seriously after retirement from a blend of several careers, ranging from broadcasting to security systems and sound system contracting to website development and hosting to teaching for the FAA drone test. He grew up reading the Hardy Boys series, along with authors like Robert Heinlein or Isaac Asimov, and exploring the works of Aldous Huxley and Bertrand Russell.

Tim studied broadcasting and media at St. Petersburg College in the late 60s while working in local television and radio. After that, he began writing radio newscasts and commercials. Fast-forward past his time in broadcasting, security contracting, teaching drone courses, video production, web design and hosting, he pub-lished several non-fiction titles before being joining a local writer's group in Daytona, Florida. A member of that group, Veronica H. Hart (*Silent Autumn, The Knife, The Prince of Keegan Bay,* and many more), encouraged him to explore fiction writing. The future promises more science fiction short stories, perhaps even a novel, as well as non-fiction work.

Tim Trott invites you to visit his website at TimTrottWrites.com.

Please consider these other books by the author:

Science Fiction/Paranormal:

The Psychic Barista (The Brown Bean Coffee Shoppe)
  Short Stories
  More Short Stories

Biography:

Out of the Blue: The Life and Legend of Kirby "Sky King" Grant,
  First Through the Fire (the story of Talbert Gray)

Education:

Understanding WordPress 6.x for Beginners
  FAA UAG 107 Remote Pilot Study Guide
  Drone Operations

Online Security:

Guarding Against Online Identity Theft
  Proteccion de Identidad

Misc/LCB:

LOTTO TRAKR